VAMPIRE WARS

THE
HOWLING

Heather Knox

EPIC Escape

An Imprint of EPIC Press
abdopublishing.com

The Howling
Vampire Wars: Book #4

abdopublishing.com

Published by EPIC Press, a division of ABDO, PO Box 398166, Minneapolis, Minnesota 55439. Copyright © 2019 by Abdo Consulting Group, Inc. International copyrights reserved in all countries. No part of this book may be reproduced in any form without written permission from the publisher. Escape™ is a trademark and logo of EPIC Press.

Printed in the United States of America, North Mankato, Minnesota.

062018
092018

Cover design by Candice Keimig
Images for cover and interior art obtained from iStockphoto.com
Edited by Jennifer Skogen

Library of Congress Cataloging-in-Publication Data

Library of Congress Control Number: 2018932898

Publisher's Cataloging in Publication Data

Names: Knox, Heather, author.
Title: The howling/ by Heather Knox
Description: Minneapolis, MN : EPIC Press, 2019 | Series: Vampire wars; #4
Summary: Delilah comes face-to-face with the past as Victor delivers her from a gruesome fate at Project Harvest: the Howling, a three-day hunt celebrated at the full moon. It's not Delilah's first Howling, though, and she knows just what a prize a Keeper would be. The captives use this distraction to stage an escape—with disastrous results.
Identifiers: ISBN 9781680769074 (lib. bdg.) | ISBN 9781680769357 (ebook)
Subjects: LCSH: Vampires--Fiction. | War--Fiction--Fiction. | Ethnic festivals--Fiction. | Prisoner-of-war escapes--Fiction | Young adult fiction.
Classification: DDC [FIC]--dc23

For Sylvia Quinn

Now

THEIR HANDS ON ME, I FEEL THE FAMILIAR PULL OF MY inner predator: teeth gnashing, claws scraping, a pressure building in my head, throbbing and buzzing, until her growl escapes my throat. Fangs bared. The woman's grip on my arm tightens and I see the bruises form before I feel the bone start to give. My growl turns to howl and rips through the foggy vellum of night.

"Mina . . . " Her brother's voice hangs heavy with warning. She rolls her eyes and lets her grip relax just slightly.

In an effort to soothe my inner predator I study

the scars that wind their way over the man's chest and arms, no doubt in my mind now that these souvenirs of ritual work must be telling of his lineage rather than Praedari tradition. His red, wavy hair hangs loose, a veil over part of his muscular chest. Both their eyes reflect the moonlight, glow amber from within as one might see in any nocturnal wild animal, but he reminds me of fireweed honey, of something growing from ash rather than being reduced to it. When he catches me staring he looks away.

"Fine, Liam. I guess it isn't much sport if I cripple her first," Mina grins, fangs sliding downwards, punctuating the promise.

My eyes linger on the jagged scar that runs from her right ear down across her throat to her clavicle and likely further. I shudder to think what could leave a scar like that on one of the Everlasting and what she could have done to walk away from it. Unlike her brother, she wears her hair done up in a series of braids and knots away from her face, loose and messy.

"It's not my place to deprive the others the thrill of the hunt on this sacred night," she smirks.

"She isn't the one chosen for the Howling, sister," Liam cautions.

"The Howling," I whisper to no one, but as soon as my breath crosses the threshold of my lips Mina hears, a Cheshire Cat smile transforming her smirk as she misinterprets my statement as a question.

"Did you hear that, brother? Our quarry is definitely a Keeper!"

Of course no Praedari would forget the full moon, this rite rumored to be as ancient as their sect. The history depends on whom you speak to, but a few theories as to origin exist. Some say the rite celebrates the rising up of Ismae the Bloody, when she turned on the Keepers' offer to be their warlord and founded the Praedari. Some say this time serves to honor our beast-self in the most primal way, indulging this aspect of ourselves rather than swallowing it down. Still smaller groups within the Praedari use this time to celebrate a goddess figure not unlike Ismae herself, hunting under the pregnant moon to honor the Becoming of the first Praedari at her divine fang and celebrating their own rebirth each month. And many younger Praedari say it only exists to strengthen the bond between packmates, the historical context lost to time and no longer necessary. And yet none of these interpretations excludes the others.

I bite my lip and narrow my eyes.

"I still think we should bring her up to the house, through intake. *Especially* if she's a Keeper," he urges, eyes darting between his sister and the path to the ranch house.

"She is why this night exists, brother. Would you forsake tradition to get in the boss's good graces?" In the absence of a response, she continues, addressing me. "Very few survive the Howling, Keeper. It is an honor to be chosen and fall for the pack."

Not all Praedari belong to a pack, but on the night of the Howling all Praedari, even the loners, come together for the revelry, for the hunt. This symbolic act of unity cements their dedication to their brothers and sisters in the sect, even if just for this night. Zeke explained once that this rite may be responsible for the formation of most packs, as many Praedari find comfort in running with one another and choose to remain bonded. The recurrence of it at each full moon strengthens this relationship, leading to a preferred pack structure throughout most of the sect. Indoctrination by experience rather than decree. The illusion of choice.

"A good death is honorable, but so is fighting honorably and *not* dying—as our sister did," Liam smirks.

"Quinn may have fought honorably, but then why not return and celebrate her victory?" Mina challenges.

Liam shrugs. Neither tenses, as though this argument has been had enough times to live outside their bodies.

Quinn? They can't mean—

"What honor is there in killing your own?" I spit, trying to keep them talking.

"Of course the symbolism is lost on you, Keeper.

But the wolves are hungry, hear their jaws snapping? You will die unremarkably and be forgotten."

"Like your sister?"

They stop dragging me.

"You little—"

But Mina's voice is blotted out by Liam's fist connecting with my cheek, the *crack!* and momentary darkness of impact. My head jerks to the side and I'm lying on the gravel of the path to the silo, sharp rocks digging into my palms and shoulder and outer thigh. I spit droplets of metallic-tasting dark onto the gravel.

"Maybe *I* killed her. Redhead, right? A little taller than you?" I ask, gesturing to Mina. "And a lot more graceful . . . " A boot to the ribs interrupts me, hard enough that I feel the familiar force of two ribs fracturing. "Or maybe she defected to the *right* side," I manage to provoke between grunts.

This time it is Liam who spits, a glob of wet landing near my eye. I wipe it away with the back of my hand.

"Shows what you know, Keeper. There was never a more loyal Praedari than Quinn."

"One hundred forty-seven Keepers killed in either single combat or outnumbering her, a branding by holy water for each on her back," Mina boasts, yanking me to my feet by my hair. "It is no surprise the Keepers do not sing tales of Saint Quinn the Shieldbreaker after she broke through their defenses in the south and led the campaign to take their territory. Keepers would never recognize the valor of one who opposed them."

"And when we cut out your tongue you won't be able to either," Liam adds, stepping towards me.

"Wait, brother—I want to hear her beg for her life. I want to hear who the Keepers pray to in their Final Moments." She tugs on my hair, pulling my ear to her lips. "The wolves may hunger, but you will be *my* kill," she hisses. "I can't wait to taste you."

Before

A POUNDING ON THE DOOR STAMPEDING OVER Tomas's voice: "Zeke! Delilah! Let's hunt us some Keeper scum!"

Several voices whoop and howl, fists also thundering on the walls of the hallway and any doors they come across, each popping open in response to add Praedari to the percussive parade.

"Are you nervous?" I ask Delilah as she pulls open the door to our shared room, our words swallowed by the ruckus.

The bed remains unmade, the only light from a bare-bulb lamp on the nightstand, drapes drawn shut and duct-taped to the wall forming a gunmetal gray rectangle. The rest of our pack likewise bunkered in neighboring rooms, only Tomas made a show of trying to room with us and even that half-heartedly. The others tacitly respect the privacy I've claimed for us since her Becoming—easily enforced locally, but more fragile at the larger Praedari gatherings. A cover maintained by the local packs, this halfway house emptied two days ago to serve as lodging for those traveling for the Howling. Residents who kept clean will undoubtedly serve as refreshments, but I do not mention this to her. The blood of those that didn't will fetch a high price to thrill-seekers, Praedari and Keepers alike.

"Why would I be?" The resolve of her voice is undermined by a glance towards the noisy serpentine S of Everlasting snaking around the corner, pushing into one another, laughing, clapping one another on the back.

"Yes, you are."

She shrugs. "Why ask a question you know the answer to?"

"Their alpha tells me they captured a Keeper operative infiltrating one of their packs," I explain carefully, unnecessarily because I know she already knows, but I want her to reflect on this a moment before we enter into the Howling. "That pack faced execution for their stupidity, and the one they captured will be our quarry tonight."

Her expression thoughtful, I know she's considering the weight of each word. The walls have fangs so we've mastered a sort of doublespeak in enemy territory. I wait a couple seconds for the hardening of her jaw, a furrow of her brow, a slight nod indicating she understands but it does not come so I continue.

"Let's show our appreciation for their hospitality the *Praedari* way," I add.

She dips her chin in a quick nod of understanding. *No mercy* but I needn't say it. Should we be the first to stumble upon the chosen for the Howling it will be Delilah's first Keeper kill. The Praedari consider it an honor when a chosen brother or sister dies for the hunt—but even greater the honor for a brother or sister blessed with a Keeper kill during the rite.

She will kill not for honor, but because it is kill or be killed. She will kill because she must understand the fragility of our place amongst the Praedari, that one misspoken word or ill-timed gesture could be the end. And she will kill because she must learn how expendable we are to our own kind, to the Keepers we risk our unlives for. Neither the Praedari nor the Keepers will mourn this loss of life. No funeral will catch the tears of those who continue to rise each night. That is not the way of the Everlasting.

I could protect her from this but I do not.

3

Now

"T HE VIBE IS WEIRD HERE TONIGHT," KILEY announces to her suitemates, looking up from the papers she and Logan pour over, the two sprawled on her bed. Amongst their mess a game, Pandemic Legacy, the box open at the foot of the bed.

"Yeah, like what's all that howling?" Charlie asks, pretending to pour over the thick rule book from her own bed next to Kiley's.

"Remember? They were talking about the full moon last time we listened in, but we got cut off before we figured out why. Something about having a lot of visitors for a few nights? Anyway, there's been

more activity than usual in this quadrant tonight—
must be what they were talking about," Hunter
explains from the door to the suite where he's been
studying the video screen, as he has been most nights,
taking notes.

"*Quadrant?*" Kiley rolls her eyes.

"You don't think—no. No way, right?" Charlie
half-asks, eyes wide.

"Hmm?" Logan cocks his head at the question she
didn't finish asking, as if to encourage her to speak up.

"You don't think there's werewolves, do you? I
mean, if vampires exist—and obviously they do—but
they'd be enemies, right? Werewolves and vampires
are enemies?"

Hunter rolls his eyes. "Sure. And maybe you'll
fall in love with a dark and brooding vampire boy
who sparkles in the sun. In fact, maybe he'll even ask
you to prom!" he mocks with a squeal and clap of
fake delight, sending the notebook he was writing in
sprawling. He follows it to the floor, scooping it up,
his cheeks flush with embarrassment. He avoids eye

contact with the others, returning his gaze to the video screen.

"Hey, she has a point," Logan defends. "Vampires existing kind of blows open the possibility of everything *else* existing . . ."

"Forget that for right now. We gotta focus," Kiley snaps.

"Are you sure this is going to work?" Charlie asks.

"No."

"You couldn't even lie to me about that?" Charlie drops the rule book and lets her head fall back on the pillow as she flops onto her back with a sigh.

"What's the point? Whatever happens it won't be worse than this."

"Famous last words," Charlie mutters.

"You have a better plan?" Kiley challenges.

"Logan, back me up here," Charlie implores.

"No way. I'm not getting into a debate with Kiley on this," he says, throwing his hands up in surrender. "I haven't had enough coffee. Besides, it's a good plan."

"A good plan?"

"Well, it's not a *bad* plan . . . "

"It's the only plan we've come up with," Hunter barks from near the door.

"I just mean that it's a rather naive way to think," Charlie offers, fingering the game tokens. "We're all alive, fed, showered, sheltered, even entertained." She tosses one of the tokens into the small compartment in the box on the next bed over. It clinks as it joins the others. Kiley raises an eyebrow at the impossible shot. "It could get a lot worse. If we wait—"

"And how many times have you been kidnapped by vampires, exactly?"

"Well, never."

"Doing something always feels better than doing nothing," Kiley says.

"Besides, they need us alive or we'd be dead already. It's not a sure bet, but it's time to play our hand," Logan adds.

"Could you guys just shut up already!?" Hunter hisses as he waves them over.

On the screen Lydia's packmate, Pierce, speaks to a man none of them have met but have seen before on the screen in passing. Pierce gestures wide with his hands before putting them on the shoulders of the man in front of him. Hunter drops to his knees below the screen and puts his finger to his lips to signal to the other three to be quiet before he pushes and holds down a button. The other three drop to their knees and crawl to him.

"A bloody Keeper!? Are you serious?" Pierce's excited whisper comes through the speaker.

With the volume turned almost all the way down, Hunter discovered that they can eavesdrop with minimal chance of being found out—as long as they crouch below the camera on their end of the video screen and don't make a sound. And as long as whoever is in the hallway doesn't notice the inside of the suite appearing on the outside screen. They've been busted on it a couple times, since the cameras in the suite are monitored periodically—but only periodically since they've proven themselves contented guests, if restless. Would've been messy but Lydia intervened on their behalf the last time. *Come on, it's gotta get boring in there,* she persuaded. *Besides, I don't think they're stupid enough to do it a second time,* and Kiley assured her they weren't. It's not a perfect system, but it's something.

"Yeah, man! Mina and Liam got her, found her prowling around outside," the man explains.

"That could've been me and Lydia if we weren't stuck babysitting," Pierce laments. "Think Victor would notice if we left our post?"

"Actually, I'm looking for him—you know how he wants us to handle intruders, figure I'd save Mina and Liam the hassle of intake."

"He might be with Ismae," Pierce offers. A second passes before he adds with a laugh: "Calm down, she's still asleep."

"Asleep or not—" the man cuts himself off, lowering his voice. "She's scary. I'll let the Viking twins—"

But Hunter lets his hand move from the button.

"What!? Come on—" Kiley reaches upwards for the button but Hunter snatches her wrist.

"We got enough. You know we can't risk being busted again." His eyes bore into Kiley's. "Your girlfriend won't cover for us forever," he adds.

Kiley tenses.

"Shut up, Hunter," Logan warns.

"Not *girlfriend* girlfriend. We know you've got dibs, buddy," Hunter turns and smirks at Logan.

"You better hope the vampires get here before—" Logan leans forward but Charlie puts a hand on his chest to stop him.

Logan glares at Charlie, then stands.

"I need coffee," he grumbles, heading into the adjoining kitchenette.

"You wanted a distraction, Kiley," Charlie pipes up, trying to diffuse the situation. "This Keeper or whatever might be it—but your plan didn't account for something."

"What's that?"

"Weapons."

4

Now

"IF WE'RE GONNA TAKE ADVANTAGE OF THIS DISTRAC-tion we'll have to go without weapons," Hunter mumbles through his last mouthful of Cocoa Puffs.

"No way. Not if I have anything to say about it!" Charlie scoffs, whipping her head to shoot him a spoon-melting glare for even suggesting such a thing.

"Whoa, alright. The NRA called, they want their spokeswoman back," he jokes, rising from his chair to take his bowl to the sink.

"What hurts them?" Logan asks, already on his way to the kitchenette himself.

"The sun—otherwise I have no idea," Hunter suggests.

"Not guns," Charlie chimes in, shaking her head.

"Holy water, garlic, wooden stakes, crucifixes," Kiley begins listing.

"Did Lydia tell you that?" Hunter asks, more an insult than a question.

"No. Movies," Kiley shrugs.

"Movies?"

"You got a better idea?"

"Well, cross garlic off the list," Logan calls from the kitchenette, just before appearing in the doorway holding a mesh produce bag of garlic bulbs. "Hey! Who polished off the Twinkies?" he grumbles.

"Why?"

"They're my favorite. You guys know that," Logan groans loudly from the kitchenette.

"No, I mean why should we cross garlic off the list," Kiley sighs, rolling her eyes.

"They wouldn't give it to us if it hurt them."

"By that logic wood must not hurt them either,

then," Charlie adds, gesturing around the room: wooden nightstands, wooden chairs.

"Huh. I felt pretty good about that one, too," Kiley pouts. "Holy water feels pretty real, doesn't it?"

"This isn't something we should be guessing at," Hunter groans.

"Hunter is right. We're better off unarmed than armed with the wrong stuff," Charlie warns.

"How do you figure?"

"Armed with nothing, you'll rely on yourself: your wits, your strengths, your cunning. Armed with a weapon, you'll rely on *it*."

"What's that from?"

"My dad . . . " Charlie answers with a frown before biting her lower lip.

"What about holy water?"

"What about it? It's a guess *and* a moot point unless one of you moonlights as a priest."

"Well, *technically* holy water is just water that is blessed. The source of the water, the specifics of the blessing, and who can do the blessing depend on the religion."

"Why do you know that?"

"Catholic high school. We had this new Religions teacher last year who took the S on the end literally. She didn't last long."

"Okay, if we're relying on a weapon that may or may not work, it's *not* going to be maybe-holy, maybe-not water. I vote wooden stakes," Hunter argues. "You two are working in the yard tomorrow night, aren't you?" he asks, addressing Charlie and Logan.

Charlie gives a half-nod. "Consider it done."

"Even if that's right, how are we going to get a sharpened stick through the *heart* of one of them? I can't say for sure, but I imagine it's not like a hot knife through butter."

Charlie bites her lower lip again, thinking. "Maybe you guys can't—but I think I can."

5

Now

BEFORE THE DOORS TO THE CONVERTED SILO OPEN, I hear the bedlam from within: shouting, grunting, chanting, laughing, the splintering of wood, metal on metal. A howl goes up, a single voice echoed by a chorus, the same pitch and duration. One long howl followed by three shorter yips. Only because of my time with Praedari do I recognize this howl as the last rallying cry for all who hear it. One by one, voices join the cacophony in acknowledgment. Mina, Liam.

From the direction of the ranch house, about a half dozen other voices. I can't distinguish one from the other except to know that I'm outnumbered in both locations, but far less so towards the house. That I see no movement between us and the house tells me that there's something important enough for at least one pack to miss the Howling, an absence no loyal Praedari takes lightly, though at times necessary.

Weathered barn doors slide open with grunts from within. Heavy steel throws up sparks as the bottom drags along a metal track, the inside of the doors reinforced, just one of many improvements apparent once the doorway yawns open. At the center, a bonfire roars, spitting glowing embers haphazardly. Spiral staircases hug the wall of the silo to both the left and right leading upwards, dotted with stark viewing platforms. I concentrate on where they meet: a larger platform from which a shirtless man, muscled, with dark, bloody war paint glistening in the firelight, stands, holding up a pewter-colored chalice adorned with etchings that match his war paint. Blood splashes from the chalice down his arm to his feet but he does not notice. Tonight he will lead the dozens assembled here in the Howling.

The words that fill the space are not English but guttural, at once the cosmic source of language and more than language: the ancient Praedari tongue, known by few and spoken by fewer. Eyes widen but none dare whisper. The cadence the same, they all know the incantation as well as they know their own heart's blood, having heard or uttered it every full moon since their Becoming—but the man pauses all the same, nodding to another a few platforms lower.

"Brothers and sisters!" this second man echoes in translation, "The full moon is upon us! And with it, the rite of the Howling."

Feet stomp on the wooden platforms along the staircase, the sound reverberating throughout the silo, a familiar vibration I feel in my bones. With a sharp crack one splinters, sending three men and three women sprawling. A few gasps rise from the crowd, their own voices hooting and hollering as they fall, cheering from others as they spring again to their feet. Only Liam and Mina maintain their composure, neither's lips so much as twitching towards a smile.

My attention stays with the Ritemaster, his lips pursed in tacit disapproval. As he waits for silence to spread over those assembled, he scans the room, his eyes stopping when they meet mine. His intensity reminds me of Enoch, the eldest of the Council of Keepers and surely the keeper of more than one secret language, though I doubt this man to be nearly as old. Perhaps mentored by an Elder? Though the Praedari pay considerable lip service to deconstructing such formalities, such relationships do emerge—particularly where the Great Rites are concerned.

He speaks, breaking our shared gaze to address the rest of the room. His translator waits for a nod of permission before continuing.

"Is there one chosen for the Hunt?"

A man steps forward. "Tonight I have no name for I am the chosen for the Hunt," he announces stiffly, rehearsed.

"An honor, your sacrifice, and all honored in witnessing it. Though you have no name, your brothers and sisters shall never forget your scent. Is there any who would contest his right to be Hunted?"

Mina lets go of me and steps forward.

"I contest not his right to be Hunted, but offer another take his place."

"Who are you to speak in this sacred chamber?"

"I am Wilhelmina," she starts, her voice filling the silo, unfaltering. "Daughter of Sigurd, granddaughter of Sighild, great-granddaughter of Ragnhild, and thus my lineage continues. Pure of blood, fierce of heart, Blooded and Bonded in honor." Each of these last three phrases punctuated by her right fist connecting with her chest with a hollow *thunk*. "We, loyal Praedari, since the first of our Bloodline and until the last."

And then I see her, unfurling from the shadow cast by Mina that flickers in time with the flames. Only slightly taller than her sister, Quinn also beats her chest three times, each time the impact crashing in my ears like wave on rocks. I glance around but no one seems to notice, all eyes transfixed on either the Ritemaster or Mina or me.

"By whose authority do you offer this proxy?" The man translates.

"By my own."

The Ritemaster raises his chalice towards her, as if in toast, and sips, a gesture recognizing her status as either alpha or loner, no matter to him—just a formality. Liam shoves me forward in response. The other Praedari do not stir. Even the nameless chosen dare not move a muscle. I, as most, have not seen this deviation from the standard rite before and do not know what comes next.

If she has not, Mina's grace fools us all as she continues, unbidden: "My brother and I found this Keeper prowling in the shadows on the property."

Liam steps forward to join his sister and me, leaving me unfettered to stand alone between them, in front of the still-open doors. I'm about a half-pace behind them, hovering, too near to run, too outnumbered to fight. My best bet is to let this play out and take the generous one hour head start offered their prey on the final night of the Howling: the Hunt. What sport in hunting something already captive? While they continue their rite—working themselves into a feral, frenzied state by continuing the Blood Games of the first two nights on the third, culminating in the Hunt—I can steal a vehicle or hide or hunker down in a small enough space that I can force them to take me on one at a time.

The fire pops, sending a shower of embers to rain down around itself, some swallowed back into the belly of the blaze. Running, hiding, fighting—futile, no matter how I spin it. But I can try to find some gasoline and flame and set fire to the main house and whatever is inside. Must be valuable, that they would miss a night as sacred as this to tend to the house. The Quinn no one but me sees melts into a foot-sized blood-smear on the concrete. I'll die as those who went before, but not in vain. I just wish I had a cell signal, so that I could send Caius and the Council my location, a goodbye gift from me to them, from me to this Praedari hive.

A rustling behind me. I turn to see a tar-colored bird at the threshold of the silo. *Quinn.*

Not meddling, huh? I think, but then a cheer goes up from those assembled, interrupting my anger. I turn again to Mina, Liam, the dozens of gathered Praedari, scanning for the source of their excitement. The Ritemaster does not mirror their enthusiasm, his thumb turned up in acceptance of her offering. Mina, too, maintains her composure: head tilted just slightly upwards, eyes trained forward, arms clasped behind her back. Liam claps her on the back, smiling. The cheers turn to howling.

I hear rustling again at the threshold of the silo. The tumult hushes, this time their collective gaze falling beyond us. The three of us with our backs to the door turn but even before I see I know, a phantom warmth breaking out over my skin, that mortal blush long since leached from my flesh by the Becoming. Against the night stands not a bird, but a man, his gray eyes fixed on my own and in that instant I know he can see through me—no, not through, but into, as if my skin hides as little as Saran Wrap around leftovers. For the first time tonight, surrounded by snarling beasts, I recognize that I'm not much more.

Now

SMS Failed to Send. Retry?

Caius cusses under his breath as the fingers of his good hand hit too many tiny buttons; the message he typed a nearly illegible amalgam of letters, but better than the eight other tries. Delilah regularly espoused the benefits of updating his technology but even this "burner phone," as she called it, frustrates him. He sees no sense in relying on something so fragile, so immediate; the luxury of youth. He and Zeke wrote letters to stay in touch, having mastered a way to speak the things they kept so carefully guarded from mortals' prying eyes. Even when he finally broke down and stole this phone he only used it to receive calls—mostly from Zeke.

And yet, for her he finds himself mashing on a gummy keypad with blood-stained fingers, mud-caked nails.

SMS Failed to Send. Retry?

She told him not to call, said she found herself too deep in enemy territory, didn't want to be compromised.

SMS Failed to Send. Retry?

The Council requested he contact her.

SMS Failed to Send. Retry?

Their request was less request and more demand. Temperance held them off as long as she could, he supposes, still not trusting the Siren but finding himself with no choice in the matter.

SMS Failed to Send. Retry?

He snarls and throws the thing at the half-open metal door of the bathroom stall in a dump of a bar in a nothing town, halfway between where he last knew Delilah was poking around and the Council's chambers. It splinters, pieces clattering across dingy tile, a few splashing into the toilet. He grabs the door and tears it from its hinges with a growl, as easily as a child tearing construction paper. It crashes against the mirror, shattering it, shards of glass exploding to rain down on the sink below.

The door to the bathroom swings open. A slack-jawed townie gapes at the mess, eyes darting between Caius and the scattered remains of the mirror. He says nothing as Caius brushes past him.

7

Now, and Not

"DELILAH?" THE MAN WITH THE GRAY EYES ASKS but it's not really a question.

"Who're you?" A voice from behind the wooden fence asks.

Delilah wipes tears from her eyes and looks to the direction of the voice. A pair of gray eyes set in a face about her age peers over the fence. She can see in the narrow space between the grass and the bottom of the fence that he must be standing on a lawn chair, the very bottom of its white plastic legs visible.

"Delilah. Who're you?"

"I'm Victor. We just moved in."

She'd noticed the U-Haul and grown-ups coming and going all week. Every morning at breakfast she asked her parents if they'd noticed any kids or toys or bikes or any signs of kids at all, but they hadn't. Her eyes widened. Maybe he's a ghost. But wouldn't a ghost just walk through the fence?

"Are you a ghost?" She narrows her eyes, clutching a small box wrapped in packing tape, the Amazon.com smile beaming outward, and an orange plastic shovel to her chest.

"What? You're weird. What's that?" Victor points at the box.

"My cat."

"Is it dead?"

"Yeah."

"Can I help?"

Before Delilah can answer Victor bounds away

from the fence. She sets the box and her shovel in the grass and finds the spot in the fence where the boards swing loose. Delilah and the girl who lived here before, Ruby, her best friend ever, would sneak into each other's yards this way. Ruby's family moved to Orlando last summer and Delilah supposes she probably has a pet alligator by now. Or maybe a whole family of pet alligators.

Maybe if her parents wrote to Ruby's parents they could send her a baby alligator since now it couldn't eat Waffles because Waffles is dead. Sad as she is, this makes her smile.

"Over here!" She pokes her head through the gap and waves Victor over. He drags a snow shovel through the gap and the two run over to the box.

"Can I see?" Victor asks, reaching for the box. Delilah shakes her head.

"Mom told me not to open it. Waffles has been in our garage freezer since like November because the ground was too hard."

"Waffles?"

"My cat."

"Aw, okay." And with that Victor starts digging. "You think it smells bad?"

"Probably," Delilah shrugs and crouches alongside where he stands, working her beach shovel into the dirt, wiggling it back and forth and back, while Victor steps on the snow shovel, using his weight to gouge into the ground. He stumbles a little, recovers, repeats. They work together in near-silence, Victor grunting occasionally, Delilah stealing glances up at him.

It doesn't take long for them to abandon their shovels, Delilah the first to get on her knees and dig into the wet, soft earth with her hands.

8

Now

I AM SIX-YEARS-OLD AND SUDDENLY I'M NOT. I breathe in dirt. Darkness and dirt. Nowhere to move dirt to because I am surrounded by it. I kick and writhe and claw. I think I scream but dirt eats the sound. I eat dirt. I breathe dirt. I become dirt. I am dirt, wet and soft.

My fingers graze something soft and cold, a different soft and cold than dirt. Waffles? But no fur, just flesh. Another buried like me but not twisting, writhing, clawing. I scream but the dirt swallows the sound. I tear at the soil, the musk of earth and decay in my nostrils.

My hand reaches through and past. Cool air. Space. Open. I claw and claw and emerge gasping, coughing, choking except I'm not and somehow I'm alive and not. I do not feel my heart racing but something inside me pulses, something besides me, something beside me. I do not feel fear. Screams: my own and another's, a woman's, as she looks into an open grave at the taped-up Amazon box which is really the smooth polished top of a coffin that's not really there and neither is she. I cannot tell which screams echo in my head and which resonate in the night. I cannot tell which are my own. I lunge towards something once-warm and slow. That is the heart I do not hear, but the thing inside me senses this thing beside me that I rake with fingernails.

I lunge but this something, the temperature of night, blurs away. I am aware that someone speaks but I do not understand. A part of me not me—but, at the same time, all of me—growls and lunges again. I hit the ground hard. No heartbeat but I smell blood. My own, another's—and his and his. Everything echoes. I breathe deeply and attempt to focus and it burns as I push down this old-new part of me that growls and lunges and isn't me. Swallowing instinct, impulse, I sputter, coughing up dirt. I am laying on the ground on my side. How did I get here? Particles of dirt and droplets of blood that aren't really there spatter the dew-soaked grass that is really concrete. The blood-smear. The silo.

Someone speaks. I groan and roll onto my back. Echoing turns to spinning. Flames. Faces. The breathy roar of dozens of whispers. A man's voice. A man kneels next to me. How long has he been there? How long has it been?

PAUSE.

It sounds familiar, right?

Dear reader, let me share with you something that, for decades, I searched for: the body does not forget. The body learns and relearns. The body might even confuse, but it will not forget. Forgetting, remembering, those are tricks of the brain, of the heart, of time; the body scars. Sometimes invisibly.

10
Now

"How long has it been?" the man with the gray eyes asks, shaking his head. He smiles. "I didn't think I'd see you again, Delilah."

I blink.

"Can you hear me?"

I nod.

He places one arm around my back and extends his other hand to me to help me sit up. I hesitate, then reach out. When my skin meets his, the world spins again, like it did when I was made by not-him, like it did the first time he kissed me that I can't remember but I know there must've been a first time, I've seen myself standing over his casket and it couldn't have been a trick. My eyes widen. He shifts and I feel his arms wrap around me. I'm trembling, becoming earthquake. This has all happened before and yet it hasn't. Then I see myself trembling in this not-stranger's embrace. I've stepped outside myself, but no, I'm here, in the present where voices spar over me.

"Why did no one tell me of her arrival?" the man with the gray eyes demands.

"How do you know her?" a woman's voice challenges. Mina.

"It's the night of the Howling, Victor," Liam begins to reason, rushing to his sister's aid, but stumbling over the words that would follow. He claps his sister on the back, attempting to diffuse the tension but she scowls at Victor.

"You were going to offer her up for the Hunt?" he asks, narrowing his eyes at the realization.

"She is a Keeper, Victor," Mina starts. "Gifted to

us by Fate for the Hunt. We must honor the Old Ways—" but he raises his hand to silence her.

The others stare, their whispers subsiding as necks visibly crane. They do not want to miss a word. Even the Ritemaster steps towards the wooden railing of the platform above all the rest, gripping it as if what is said in this next moment might determine whether he needs to tear it from its supports and shove it through a heart or ten. Victor helps me to my feet, placing himself between me and the others.

"Are you hurt?"

I shake my head no in response. He turns again to address Mina and Liam, standing somehow taller than his height, a trick of the firelight or the Blood.

"Keeper or not, you violated protocol. Under the guise of tradition you jeopardize everything we've built here," he manages from a clenched jaw. He pauses, his brow furrowing for just a shadow of a moment before he continues. "You have until the sunrise that ends the Howling."

Liam and Mina glance at one another, then again to Victor.

"You have until that sunrise to decide which of you dies."

The two men nearest us rush to Mina and Liam's sides, grabbing them each above the elbow in restraint but Victor waves them off. Mina yanks her arm from the man who grabs her, a gob of wet landing on his cheek as she spits.

"Leave them be. Let them spend their Final Moments together."

"And if they run?" the man asks, his low voice sandpaper against Victor's.

"To run would disgrace their family," he explains, his eyes not leaving Mina's.

"And if they fight?"

Victor's eyes leave Mina's to fix on Liam's. Liam tilts his head just slightly upwards, coolly, at once defiant and accepting of his fate.

"Then let them fight," Victor challenges.

11

Now

"OKAY, SO, LIKE, WHAT THEN? LET'S SAY YOU *CAN* plunge a stake into a vampire's heart, Charlie—let's say that you're strong enough because you have their magic blood or whatever in you. Then what? How do we even know that that'll work?" Hunter doubts.

The four captives occupy two of the beds, the guys lounging on and against one and the girls on the other. Hunter rests on the floor, back against the bed, knees drawn up to his chest. Logan lays on his side above him. On theirs, Kiley lays across it the short way, her legs dangling off one side and her head hanging over the other. Charlie sits cross-legged, clutching a pillow to her chest.

"A stake in the heart would kill *you*, wouldn't it?" Charlie quips.

"Obviously—but lots of things would kill me that probably don't kill them. Time. Being shot. Uhm . . . " Hunter struggles to find more examples.

"Well, there's things that probably kill them that *don't* kill us—like sunlight," Kiley offers.

"Think of it like anatomy," Logan starts. "They're animated corpses, right?"

A mixture of shrugs and nods from the others beckon him to continue.

"And . . . well, that's all I've got," Logan sighs. "For zombies, go for the head. For vampires, the heart. It's in *all* the movies."

"So we're back to that?" Hunter whines, standing and flinging a plastic tumbler against the wall. "Back to guessing?"

"Were we ever *not* guessing?" Charlie retorts, standing.

Hunter paces the length of the suite, a habit the others have found annoying since the first night they were brought here so he usually tries not to. He can almost feel the eye-rolls and he can definitely hear Kiley groan as she sits up to glare at him.

"You know that makes me anxious," she snaps.

"The heart is in all the lore, right? The movies and books and shows? A stake in the heart turns them to ash."

"I think you were maybe onto something, Logan. In us, the heart pumps blood. The right side receives . . ."

Logan waves him off. "We've all had bio, dude. Fast-forward."

"What I'm saying is, what if it's the same with vampires?"

"I'm not sure that that's the case," Charlie speaks up. "Their hearts don't beat, right? So do they pump? If not—"

"Okay, can I finish my story?" Hunter barks. "I'm *saying*, what if it's kind of like that, but for magic?"

"Magic?" Kiley crinkles her nose.

"So vampires, ghosts—both good, but magic? Magic is where you draw the line?"

"You sound like Lydia." She rolls her eyes.

"Hunter might be onto something," Logan offers. "And it's the best theory we've got."

Hunter stops his pacing to face them. "Too bad there's not a way to do the same thing with the electricity in this place."

"But there is!" Charlie jumps up from the bed, tossing the pillow to the floor but Hunter is in its trajectory and takes a face full of feathery fluff. "And I think I know how to do it . . . "

12

Now

VICTOR GUIDES ME FROM THE SILO. I HADN'T REAL-
ized how near the surface my predator within
keeps vigil until I smell the dew on the grass as we
step outside, smell the cold. I am fight or flight and
the night offers such beautiful monsters.

"They're . . . intense," I start, feigning an interest
in small talk to drown out the thunder of my pupils
dilating, the panting of the beast inside me begging
to be let out for just a taste. Every silent thing in my
body echoes inside me like sea crashing into sea cave
and I can't tell what someone else might hear.

"You heard her cite her lineage?" he asks, either

having listened in or aware of how the rite unfolds when a proxy is offered.

I nod.

"They're pure bloods, a rarity amongst Everlasting. They only Usher from their mortal bloodline, which dates back centuries. When she says she is the great-granddaughter of Ragnhild, she means both by blood and by *the* Blood. Liam, Wilhelmina, and Quinn shared a womb *and* a grave."

"Quinn?" Where once there was sea inside me, now a tempest rages.

"Yeah, they don't talk about her much and I never met her," he explains. "Most of the Everlasting here think Liam and Mina are twins but they're really two-thirds of a set of triplets. They joined us just over a year ago, but I couldn't tell you where from. Kept to themselves, showed no interest in expanding their pack."

Palpable, my disappointment, but I'm quick to fill the silence left by my frown.

"But you know their lineage?"

"Hard not to," he laughs. "Their pride led to more than a few shield-bashing contests—which doesn't sound like much, but they put down more than a few skilled fighters before people finally left them alone."

"You already speak of them in the past tense."

"Aren't they as good as? The sun will rise twice more before consuming one of them," he states, a punishment as old as the Everlasting, his expression unchanging in the moonlight. "One will be lost without the other. It doesn't matter who chooses to die to save the other, the survivor dies, too, the slow death of grief. They are two faces of the same moon."

I think about the moon: waxing, full, waning—but even those paint an incomplete cycle, void of nuance, illustrative at best. What of the dark moon? I want to ask about their third, about Quinn. What have Liam and Mina lost in her absence? What pieces of her do her brother and sister hold? Is she both their full moon and their dark?

"Delilah, why are you here?" Softer than a challenge, his eyes lock with mine. In that moment I feel something inside him stir, stalking the edges of the gray of his eyes, sharpening claws in the hollow of his chest, at the ready but waiting.

I could call upon my Blood and provoke, but instead I clench my fists at my sides, my fingernails pressing into the pale flesh, sending ribbons of pain into the soft tissue there, the sharpness grounding me in the moment, a trick I learned to keep myself from slipping into vision or the murky water of memory. The illusion of control.

"You—you're dead," I sputter, staring ahead at the farmhouse we're approaching, its coziness bathed in moonlight. Despite the cool light, the doorway beckons, a thing of memory living just beyond the reach of recollection.

"So're you," he says lightly. Then, glancing at my hands: "You're angry."

"I saw your body . . . "

"Did you?" When his eyes meet my glare, he continues. "I'm not being cruel, I'm asking. I was Slumbering."

"Yes. No. I mean, it was a closed casket, but I looked. Or it was open. Yes, it was open—I think—your mother cried. She screamed at me because she saw me peek but I was leaving something inside . . ."

The landscape blurs and I feel the earth below me pitch and rock, but it does neither. Sanguine crescent moons erupt on the skin of my palms. My own metallic scent hangs in the air.

"Shhhh. We don't have to do this now."

"Yes! We do!" I snap. "You're dead."

He sighs. "My Usher insisted we stage my funeral. It was risky, actually being inside the casket, especially for the burial."

He studies me. I feel the gray of his eyes like storm clouds, the way they roll in and the air around you changes. An electricity, a dampness that seeps into your skin, your lungs.

"Delilah, why are you here?"

"I—I really don't know . . ."

Not a lie, not really. I found Zeke's killer and I let her go so I could come here to find—to find what, exactly? To see if the truth is a lie, a lie the truth? But I can't think about that right now.

"Wait," I start, grasping for a distraction—as much for myself as for him. "They buried you alive? Well, you know . . . "

"Wasn't the first time, right?" He smiles.

"What?" I snap, sounding more defensive than I'd like. Could he know we were made the same way?

"You've heard the rumors about how Praedari are Ushered," he says, waving it off. "It's not untrue, but it's more elegant than you Keepers think."

Perhaps my pack played to perception, then, the Keeper part of me challenges—but he's right. All Everlasting experience a rebirth, but only the Praedari rise up from the dirt to claim their place in the pack. The Keepers trade titles and favors like trinkets, hiding behind formality, often ensuring their survival for centuries without ever stepping into the trenches; meanwhile the Praedari *build* the trenches from the bodies of their fallen brothers and sisters. I want to tell him that I know, that I, too, clawed my way from the earth—but this seems the only thing he doesn't know of me so instead I hold my tongue, guard this precious truth as if it may become weapon.

"You let me believe you were dead," I mumble, my voice swallowed by the enormity of the night.

"How many people from your past think you're dead, Delilah? We do what we have to—to survive, to protect those we leave behind."

I am silent not because he has a point, but because I do not know.

So he continues: "I didn't stay away entirely, though. I don't remember when, exactly, but I looked you up. I couldn't find you at first and it became an obsession. Eventually I found the place you used to *work*," he says, the words sticking to his tongue like honey.

"Is that judgment from someone who Huck Finned his own funeral?"

"Not at all," he deflects, throwing his hands up in surrender. "They told me you used to sing using your real name, that—"

"—stage names are for people hiding from something," we both say in unison.

13

Before

I LINGER IN THE DRIVER'S SEAT, HANDS STILL CLUTCH-ing the steering wheel. The black of my dress melts like shadow into the cracked black leather of the interior of the car and I wish I could stay in here forever, pause time so I don't have to climb out, put one foot in front of the other until someone pulls the door open for me and I step inside.

Looming in front of me, the white chapel at the town center so small that cars line all adjacent streets, forcing some mourners to walk a few blocks to pay their respects. It's the chapel his grandmother and grandfather were married in, the chapel his mother and father were married in, the chapel he grew up attending and would have someday been married in—more out of tradition than belief. The pink flowering crab apple trees on the plot served as the backdrop for photos marking each of these occasions and countless other baptisms, weddings, and funerals.

People file into the chapel, some passing me and glancing inside. A sad half-smile and a tilt of the head, but I cannot return the gesture, aware only peripherally of their presence. In here I'm armored from the condolences, exempt from the expectation that my lips offer what my heart can't yet fathom.

I jolt upright and yelp when a knock on my door startles me. Victor's mother opens my door, leaning in to hug me tightly before I know what's happening. She smells heavily of roses, her hair perfectly pinned underneath a wisp of the black lace veil attached to the black felt pillbox hat I've only ever seen her wear as part of her mourning dress. I reach awkwardly, seatbelt still buckled, to wrap my arms around her, enjoying the warmth of her embrace. She does not cry, nor does she say anything—a small blessing, the exhaustion of grief.

I was in Victor's room waiting for him to get home, reading when the police knocked. I crept to his bedroom door, peered through the crack to see his mother talking to two uniformed officers. Sometimes the body knows something before the heart does, or maybe it's the heart that's able to hear the whispers of tragedy before they pass the message bearer's lips— either way, I stepped into the living room as if on autopilot, crossed to the front door in time to catch her as she spun around, sobbing herself unsteadily into my arms. *We're sorry, ma'am. We're sorry.*

"Come inside, Delilah." She beckons, finally relaxing

her arms and pulling back to stand upright again outside the car. "It's time to say goodbye."

I nod and climb from the car, one of the black heels I wore to prom not long enough ago catching. Victor's father steadies me, one arm easily around my back and his hand on my forearm. I let him guide me inside. I nod my head, feel my lips curl into the slight upturn that can only be described as the ghost of a smile, my vocal cords vibrating with *too soon*s and *thank you*s, responding to things I know are said but cannot pierce my grief to find the part of my brain that processes language.

Sunlight through stained glass and Victor's mother takes my hand to pull me to the front of the nave of the chapel. The casket lay open: photographs, trophies, a Rubik's Cube, a flood of college acceptance letters, stuffed animals, cards from birthdays and graduation, letters written for the occasion, drawings from the youngest members of the family. I slip one hand into the pocket of my black wool peacoat, fingers fumbling with the cool of something within.

My other hand grips the casket rail until my knuckles whiten. His mother's arm linked through my own, I feel her sob gather in her chest as her muscles tense, just moments before her wailing rises above the din of reminiscing from the others gathered.

His father guides her from the casket leaving me alone. I remove my hand from my pocket, fingering the small object before slipping it between folds of the silk lining within. I take a deep breath as I turn, the cloying smell of lilies sticking in my throat.

∽✌∾

The Lord is my shepherd; I shall not want.

He maketh me to lie down in green pastures: he leadeth me beside still waters.

He restoreth my soul: he leadeth me in the paths of righteousness for his name's sake.

Yea, though I walk through the valley of the shadow of death, I will fear no evil: for thou art with me; thy rod and thy staff they comfort me.

Thou preparest a table before me in the presence of mine enemies: thou anointest my head with oil; my cup runneth over.

Surely goodness and mercy shall follow me all the days of my life: and I will dwell in the house of the Lord forever.

Amen.

೯೬

"Do not stand at my grave and weep," I start, my voice trembling into a microphone that crackles as I shuffle the paper I read from. I clear my throat as quietly as I'm able before I continue.

"I am not there, I do not sleep."

೯೬

I stare at my reflection in the full-length mirror. I've been practicing this poem for two hours, my voice catching on a different word each time. I step towards myself, lean so my forehead rests on my reflected forehead. Tears stream down my cheeks, silent sobs wracking my body. I'm vaguely aware of the emptiness of my stomach as I slump to the floor.

We'd read the poem in English class our freshman year. The poem, by Mary Frye, was never published by the poet, nor by a press—something about that near-anonymity spoke to me at the time, a certain romance in a woman writing one poem her entire life and scrawling it on a torn-off bit of paper bag. I loved Victor long before I let him know, and spent the next few months trying to find the words to scrawl onto a torn-off bit of paper bag to tell him.

It never came to me, but it didn't need to. Victor found the courage to speak his feelings long before I did. Even now I couldn't think of anything but this woman who found herself so moved by another's loss that she could write this poem. Without him, my tongue refuses to dance the syllables I know so well by heart. Without him, what need have I for language?

When I wake, I find my black dress pressed and

draped carefully over the back of the chair in the corner. My black heels rest on the floor next to the chair. My mother laid out earrings and a necklace, but I do not bother putting them on. I do not brush my hair, but when I smooth my dress in the mirror, my reflection does the same.

It's just us now.

৶৻৶

"I am the starshine of the night," I read aloud, the tell-tale pressure of the welling-up of tears in my eyes echoed in my chest. I take a deep breath to steady my voice as the next couplet begins: "I am in the flowers that bloom. I am in a quiet room."

No one stirs as a sob rips from my chest and fills the nave, so loud I swear it has manifest, the pressure in my chest releasing before knotting again. Several more follow, apparitions filling in what little space remains in the pews. Those sobs I am nearly able to swallow into silence find their way out through my

70

voice. The final line of the poem hangs over those gathered, a sort of veil; the thing everyone thinks in the throes of grief, no matter how irrational.

"Do not stand at my grave and cry. I am not there, I did not die."

Dear reader, do you want to know what I thought important enough to leave in his casket? Me, too.

15

Now

"**W**HAT DO YOU *MEAN* YOU CAN'T GET IN TOUCH with her?" Temperance demands.

"I mean that she's somewhere where she can't risk her cover being compromised."

"This isn't supposed to be some undercover op!" she hisses.

Temperance begins pacing the foyer of the downtown mansion she's had restored, one of a few historical buildings she's rescued through the foundation she started decades ago as a cover for her other endeavors. Her hands clasped behind her back, she's not dressed for company: a lace-edged silk slip the color of merlot hugs her ample curves, a matching short silk robe undone overtop. Caius shifts his weight from one blood-stained workboot to the other, avoiding looking directly at her out of modesty.

"Ezekiel used to pull this on the Council from time-to-time—he got away with it because of his status. She won't be as lucky," she warns.

"But Delilah has *his* status to back her claim. He was her Usher, after all," Caius offers.

She shakes her head. "The Council will not see it that way. She is autonomous; her actions—as well as her status—are her own."

"As I recall, Siren, *you* granted her autonomy," Caius growls.

"Don't put this on me. You're the one who lost her. As I see it, I *saved* you—we both knew she'd pull something like this. She's her Usher's Childe, after all."

"Saved me?" he scoffs. "Don't pretend you're doing anyone but yourself favors, Siren."

"Actually I did us *and* her a favor. She just hasn't figured it out yet."

"Oh yeah? What's that?" Caius challenges.

"Before she left I gave her something—a beacon of sorts that doesn't rely on technology. She just needs to see it for what it is."

"You didn't tell her what it was you were giving her?"

"It was better she not know."

Now

"NO ONE THERE LIKED YOU MUCH, BUT THEY SAID your face was plastered on every bus shelter within a few miles for a while, maybe a year," Victor explains. "That was pretty deep in Praedari territory so I assumed the worst. I tried to find some locals but those packs were laying low, not too trusting of outsiders after something took down the strongest of their packs."

How had he not put it together? Or is he toying with me, seeing how far I'll let him go before I implicate myself? The strongest pack in the region—Tomas and the others—the raid, the Howling, how that

Keeper operative they captured led them straight to the warehouse. Funny that what Zeke and I would be remembered for far beyond our Final Moments became the exact thing that allowed me to die forgotten the first time.

"Anyway, after attending your own funeral it's hard to believe anyone 'just' goes missing," he shrugs.

"Sometimes people go missing that don't want to be found." Something I'd heard before. The homeless man in the alley?

"And yet, here you are. After all these years." His lips curl into the easy smile I've known a thousand times, never quite forgetting, never quite remembering. The corners of his eyes crinkle, the wrinkles a map to a place I've taken shelter in, though I've long since lost the key. His strong nose, like the homeless guy had said—had he always hated his nose? Warmth breaks out over my cheeks and I look away a moment, hiding the flush, a gesture he could mistake for reminiscence.

Then I look him in the eyes: "Are you going to kill me?" I shoot straight with it.

"Kill you?" His voice cracks with the question and he shakes his head slightly. His brow furrows. He frowns.

"You sentenced your own to die," I add.

"Liam and Mina violated protocol, a provision we have in place for the protection of everyone here. If we just killed every Keeper that discovered our facility we'd never learn who's sending them, or their firepower, or what they know," he explains, the cadence suggesting a rehearsed response, at least in part.

"So you've caught other Keepers?"

"Just you." His answer comes quick, just as a lie might—just as the truth might.

"And you plan to keep me prisoner because you think I'm a spy?"

He sighs. "Delilah, I am not punishing Liam and Mina because they disobeyed me—I'd be killing my own men weekly were that the case. Praedari are not by nature obedient. We aren't asked to be, not in the way you guys are." He rushes to add: "Sorry. As Praedari, we're praised more for breaking rank and questioning authority than the Keepers are—some say it's how the Praedari *became* Praedari and the Keepers *became* Keepers, that a woman told the ruling Everlasting to kiss off, essentially."

He speaks of my Usher's Usher, of Ismae the Bloody, of the story Zeke told me time and time again. I don't say this, instead I merely offer a nod as if hearing this story for the first time or the hundredth, either way more interested in the fate that awaits Liam and Mina—and this man who assigned it.

"Anyway," he continues, "one of them will die because of how they treated you. Otherwise, you'd be in constant danger here. At least this way, should you choose to stay, the others will think twice about hassling you."

"Should I choose to stay?" I echo, the possibilities of the question resonating where once my heart beat.

"You're not a prisoner. You're welcome to leave whenever you like, or stay as a guest."

"But I'm a Keeper."

"So? You think your Elders don't know our location? Our numbers? Our mission? It's safe to always assume the other side knows more than you think they do, and more than you want them to."

"Then why haven't they done anything?"

He considers the question a moment, before shrugging.

"Maybe we're not really a threat to them at the moment. Maybe they want us to succeed first so they can make their move after for maximum impact, or maybe they want us to eat our own tail. Maybe they want to preserve and build upon what we've done here," he offers with an ease that makes me think he's thought this through more than once. "The bottom line is that we—the Praedari and the Keepers—are at war. It's like chess: we all know where the kings are and we all know what pieces are in play. So they wait."

"For what?"

"The answer to that holds more weight for you than for me, Delilah. I am merely their enemy; you are their agent. I know what comes for me."

Silence, the rest of the walk: through the door, into the cocoon of bright light and knickknacks that suggest a life before this one. A welcome mat, well-worn, the W-E-L-C scrubbed to ghost, the O-M-E still bright. Omen, omen. Through the garage and into a part of the sprawling complex that seems too new: too sterile, too clean, too bright. A few turns of hallway and we stop walking. All this punctuated by Victor swiping a keycard or pressing a finger to a small screen until he stops us outside a large metal door without a handle after passing a few others like it. I'm not sure I could find my way back to the entrance if I wanted.

"Here's where you'll stay," he peers into a scanner and a door that seamlessly fits to the walls slides open. "For as long as you like. This section is what we consider the visitor center. With your arrival I'll bump security up to 'restricted' for this wing—usually guests and Praedari may move freely through this area—each suite only accessible to its guests and approved visitors, of course—but I'd rather not worry about you while the others adjust to your being here."

A rustic queen-size bed made of finished pallets with a tufted headboard of clean burlap; a light gray, distressed wooden nightstand; a lamp with an Edison bulb. An armoire of the same gray distressed wood. A large TV mounted to the wall directly ahead interrupts the shabby chic charm of the room; underneath, a vintage desk with a light purple wingback chair next to a large, empty bookcase. To the right of that, a door leading to a small but bright bathroom with a large mirror, clawfoot tub, toilet, and sink. Another door leads to a kitchenette with a water cooler, a small round bistro-style table and two chairs, a short countertop with a microwave, a refrigerator, a sink, and an electric stovetop.

The bed is dressed in subdued lavender sheets, not neutral but subtle, and topped with a fluffy light gray ruffled comforter, more feminine than I'm accustomed to and certainly boasting more charm and personality than my and Zeke's semi-permanent quarters in the hotel. Still, the room feels incomplete, almost as if it grieves. On the walls, empty shadow boxes.

"We do have other guests onsite, some mortal, so I ask that all Everlasting adhere to security protocol and not disturb them—their safety and comfort are important to us. Mortal staff, however, are at your disposal around the clock," he explains.

Then, his voice softening: "No matter your reason, Delilah, I'm glad you're here." He moves his hand but stops short of making contact with the small of my back, his hand instead sweeping again to gesture inside. "I'll stop by first thing tomorrow night and introduce you to your security detail. For now I ask that you stay in your suite, but if you need anything you can use the tablet to call me or other staff. The dining staff knows how to cater to mortals *and* Everlasting, so don't feel like you need to be subtle. You may speak freely here."

17

Before

*W*E CAN'T SPEAK FREELY HERE. ZEKE'S VOICE JOINS the hum of his Blood as the metallic splashes down my throat, but his lips don't move. The hard and cool of the wood of the picnic table we sit on tingles against the backs of my bare thighs where my cut-off shorts don't reach.

I part my lips to speak, but before I can, his voice again: *We move tonight.*

We don't often share Blood—a vessel, yes, or a kill, an intimate gesture between lovers or even packmates. But tonight he offers me his throat. The ground shifts underneath my feet making it difficult to stand, like trying to stay still in an inflatable bounce house surrounded by people jumping. The electricity of a lover's fingertips grazing your skin for the first time emanates from where my heart once beat. This gives way within seconds to something more feral, a pounding in my head so loud I cannot hear him moan even though I feel the vibration of it on my lips. I dig my nails into the backs of his shoulder blades. My eyes widen to match his. The blush of life washes over me even though his is dead blood.

More than once I've thought it, that the Praedari understand something about the predator within us that the Keepers will never admit: that it is as much a part of us as the Blood—not an inconvenient side effect of the Becoming, but part of what we become. Foolish, for him to offer his throat like this. Fangs-deep in his flesh, I consider what that final drop might taste like, what secrets might cross the threshold of my lips with the last of him. Dim, dimmer, dimmer still the glow of life as it wanes from his eyes.

Someday, my love, but not tonight, and he presses on

my shoulders, pushing me away from him until my fangs hover just above where they once punctured. I gasp softly when he addresses my unspoken desire for the strictly forbidden. He refers to the tradition of our lineage that an Usher offer their Childe their Heartsblood rather than their power being lost to time or, worse, usurped by another of the Everlasting. This so-called *cannibalism*, a heretical practice among both sects, the Keepers fear the knowledge of their Elders falling to undeserving youth while the Praedari fear the opposite, in a way: that their progenitors, anticipating this, may rise up to prey on their Children.

Zeke wipes a couple drops of his blood from the corner of my mouth, offering it to me. After I lick the blood from his finger, I ask him a question in my head. *You can hear my thoughts?*

He nods. *Some*, he says, *those that you project.* Zeke dips his head to kiss my shoulder. "Those backed by powerful emotion always slip through the bond," he whispers with a grin.

But how?

We share Blood, though some say the eldest of us have the ability to link with their mortal kin, too. But this gift comes at a price, Delilah, he warns. *This is the only way we can communicate safely during the raid and still maintain our cover, so for now, we are linked.*

Will you be okay?

He shrugs. *We don't have time for you to worry about me.*

I purse my lips and jerk my head in a nod, wanting to press *pause* with so many questions bubbling up inside me that I fight to not think about, not wanting to drown Zeke in a cacophony of inquiry and still entirely unsure how this works.

We're greeted by a whistle as we join the others in the parking lot of the abandoned campground. The owner more than willing to rent it to us during the off-season and not ask questions, we're guaranteed relative privacy at the conclusion of the Hunt.

"That Keeper's one lucky punk if he gets you sucking on him tonight, Delilah," Tomas cat calls.

Zeke wraps an arm around my waist, pulling me into him with a snarl in Tomas's direction. My eyeroll follows, though it's meant for the both of them. Tomas puts his hands in front of him in mock surrender.

"Easy, bro—I'm just playin'," he offers with a toothy grin, fangs almost glowing white against the black of his fitted leather jacket. "Save the rage for the Hunt."

Always the instigator, pushing buttons to see if he can get a rise from his packmates, from the predators within them. His role in the pack informal, but vital—a pack is only as strong as their weakest member so he culls, he fortifies. Zeke and Tomas have come to blows over me more than once, but I sense something between them that runs deeper than antagonism.

"How much time the Keeper got left?" I ask.

"Sixteen minutes and forty-three seconds,"

Brittany answers, not needing to consult a watch or even the position of the bright moon against the sky. "Forty-two seconds. Forty-one."

"Show off," Tomas teases, nudging her in the ribs.

"Not my fault some of us are *useful*," she quips, crossing her arms over her chest. "You ready for this, Delilah?"

I shrug.

"A Keeper. Just seems an awful big prize for your first Hunt," she explains, an edge to her voice.

"I can handle myself."

"Brittany, when're you going to lighten up on her? She's one of us now," Tomas interjects. "She's proven herself time and again."

"Has she? This should be her eighth Howling, not her first. Seems to me her boy-toy's been taking up most of her time."

This time it's my turn to snarl as I pull from Zeke and step towards her.

"Hey, she's destroyed you in bringing in recruits

since her Becoming," Tomas defends, stepping between us.

Brittany brings her hand up to shield her eyes, scanning the horizon in a wide, exaggerated sweep of her head.

"Where they at? Seems to me the only ones that climbed from the grave were put back in it a couple weeks later by that Keeper cell we brought down."

Her point made, she glowers at Tomas before turning to the others, the slapping of high-fives and cheers punctuating their graphic boasting of what's in store for their quarry tonight. He shrugs at me before joining their tale-telling.

So we're really doing this tonight? I think, glancing to Zeke.

Tonight, he confirms, inaudible to the others. *The original plan crumbled to dust when that other operative got himself caught. This way at least his death still serves our sect.*

But Without the Council's approval? I ask.

Don't concern yourself with that. Focus on your part in this.

An awful big prize for your first Hunt. She has no idea.

Now

"SHE'LL BE HERE IN A MINUTE. I THINK YOU'LL LIKE her," Victor continues as I step out of my suite to join him in the fluorescently-lit hallway. "Her pack is easily the most capable here at the facility. I lean on them a lot lately. Lost a member, though—hey! There she is!"

The hairs on the back of my neck raise, mirroring my inner predator who steps up from the void within me. The cloying scent of lilacs nearly chokes out notes of decaying autumn leaves and rain-on-pavement. Victor waves at someone but before he can stop me I am snarling and whipping around to face a familiar blur of a cropped, faded black T-shirt and an axe to grind. The girl from the alley, again all fangs and swiping, the monster within her breaching the surface yet again.

The crack of her fist connecting with my jaw, the crack either my bones or hers, no way to tell. I stumble backwards and she lunges again. I recover quickly, bending at the waist to rush her. I throw my weight into her, knocking her to the ground, my own body following hers and landing on top of her with a mutual grunt. We're a mess of thrown limbs and gnashing teeth and growls, splayed and scrambling on the cool, clinical tile.

"You killed Johnny!" she hisses, driving a knee upwards to connect with my groin.

"Did *not!*" I shriek, yanking her hair hard enough to expose her throat for just a moment before she jams a finger in my right eye with a sickening *squish*. I scream and reel backwards, tumbling to the side and crouching in an upright fetal position, hands over my eyes. I feel warmth against my throat, like live blood when it first sings down the throat of the freshly-Ushered, but on the outside of my throat, where the Stone of Nyx hangs.

The weight of her lands on my back. I reach behind my head and grab T-shirt and hair and throw her to the ground in front of me. I pin her arms and lean over her, staring her down with both eyes, whole, half my face stained in blood and the wet of aqueous humor.

"What the—?" she shrieks, eyes wide. In them, the red glow at my throat mirrored.

Someone shouts above us and hands grab at both my and the girl's arm, shoulder, hair, leg—one person, maybe two or three—but we continue kicking and flailing, the tang of blood hanging heavy in the air.

Somewhere in the shadow of my awakened predator—in my rational mind, however far from the surface it cowers—I recognize the absurdity of it: a *did/did-not* screaming match, complete with hair-pulling and eye-clawing, between two women who've only just met, at least as far as others see. The sharp of fangs in my thigh jars even this fleeting thought from my mind, but both are chased by strong sets of hands pulling her off me.

Since no one grabs me and the immediate threat no longer such, my inner predator soothes, slinking back from the surface to observe, still at the ready. Clarity of sense follows, the shouts intelligible: our names, confusion, cussing. Lydia in a hug-hold, squirming against Victor, the disadvantage of being Ushered so young obvious in this moment: though not of intimidating stature, his wiry build contains her struggle with relative ease.

I dart into my suite and let the door shut behind me, watching on the video screen as Victor drags her out of view of the camera none too gently.

Now

"**I**'VE ALREADY TOLD YOU—A SHADOW CAME UP FROM the ground and swallowed him."

Victor still had Lydia by her bicep, a constellation of bruises smattering her flesh from fighting with Delilah and being taken down and dragged into an empty guest suite by Victor, each glowing the pale green of healing underneath the stark fluorescent lighting.

"And I'm hearing you, but are *you* hearing you?"

"Let *go* of me," she snarls, yanking her arm from his grasp. "That's what happened. And she was there, Delilah was there."

"But you said someone else was there, too."

Lydia shakes her head, unsure of why he doubts her testimony when she's a known eidetiker—first as a mortal, why her Usher wished to add her to her collection, and then enhanced by the Blood at her Becoming. "Some other woman, but it doesn't matter—Delilah made the shadows swallow him. She controls the shadows. She killed Johnny!"

"Lydia, I need you to focus," Victor says in a croon, grabbing her hands and looking into her eyes. "Maybe some Everlasting can control the shadows—you know as well as I that the Blood manifests differently between lineages, sometimes even mutating within the same. Think back to that night. Did you see her do something that the shadows responded to?"

She shakes her head no.

"You said the other woman that came after you guys had already engaged with Delilah. Is it possible she and Delilah didn't know one another?"

"No," she answers quickly, then: "It all happened fast, but I could tell you exactly how it went down.

Blow-by-blow if you really want. I can tell you her hair smelled like rose and coconut. Her eye makeup was smudged like she hadn't washed it off the night before or like she'd been crying. She—" but Victor puts up a hand to stop her.

"I'm not doubting your memory, Lydia. I realize you lost a packmate that night and I would never deny you the chance for vengeance, but if there's any chance *at all* that it wasn't Delilah responsible for his death we have the chance to do something incredible here for Operation Harvest—for all Praedari. Maybe even for all Everlasting."

Lydia narrows her eyes. "She's a Keeper. Why do you trust her?"

Victor pauses a beat before answering, his pupils dilating slightly. "I knew her a long time ago, before she was a Keeper."

"Before she was a Keeper, huh? You're made and then you are, there's no *before*."

"Come on Lydia, we both know who Ushered you. You know that's not true."

"That's different."

"I need you to trust that this is different, too. You two have some common ground."

"Doubtful," Lydia snorts but she recognizes the setting of his jaw, the slight narrowing of his eyes and soft gaze focused behind her.

"In fact," he starts after a moment, "her Usher was well-respected in their sect before he died. He probably knew Temperance."

"Victor, no," she pleads, anticipating his request.

"Temperance sits on their Council of Keepers. All I'm asking is that you spend some time with Delilah as her security detail. Talk to her. See what comes up."

"How do you know that about Temperance? Aren't their identities kept quiet?" Lydia asks.

She could feel more surprise with his admission but to be honest, she doesn't often think of her Usher, save for recently. Confiding in Kiley about Aurelie the other night was the first time she'd spoken her lost friend's name aloud in a long while; it only seemed natural that she'd feel Temperance's presence imme-diately after. Still, it bothers her she cannot shake it, as if the Blood has somehow infected her with memory—perfect memory after perfect memory, ad infinitum.

Most Everlasting sleep the dreamless sleep of death, as if revisiting their mortality each day might atone for the gift-curse of walking as one of the undead each night. But not Lydia. Lucid dreaming, some might call it, though hers are not dreams, but memories—perfect in every detail and vivid—haunt-ing her slumber, often such that her predator within cannot risk letting down her guard. While others find a sort of sanctuary in the daylight hours, Lydia and her shadow-self find themselves drowning in every scent and sound and touch from their past, aware enough to yearn for dusk and trapped until it arrives.

"Private, not *secret*," he offers. "You don't end up an Elder if you can't protect yourself—same for serv-ing on the Council when your identity leaks. Besides, the Siren's never been great at keeping a low profile."

"So you knew Delilah's Usher?"

"Not as such. At least, I didn't know he was her Usher until recently. I knew her when she was mortal, but . . . " He pauses, as if unsure how to explain their connection. "Well, we lost touch before her Becoming."

"Did you kill him?" she asks, head cocked to the side.

"I promise you I didn't," he assures her, as if the question might hold more gravity than she thought upon asking it, piquing her interest. "But I met him when he made himself known to me. I didn't realize he was her Usher until after, when I started asking questions. The Seeker, they called him. He had something I needed, and I had something he wanted."

"What did he want?"

"Information."

"About what?"

Victor shrugs. "You can ask Delilah if you're feeling brave, though I wouldn't recommend it. She carries his legacy now."

"Why are you honoring the memory of some Keeper you didn't even know?"

"You can respect the enemy even if you don't agree with them. They called him the Seeker because he sought out the forgotten lore of the Everlasting—lore that was as much his as ours."

"You sound like Liam and Mina," Lydia retorts, rolling her eyes. "'The old way's *this* and 'respect and honor' *that*," she imitates, mimicking Mina's stern demeanor with only marginal success, betraying how little she actually listened to them. "But I don't get *why* he made himself known to you? Did he know you had whatever this information was?"

"Nothing with the Keepers is coincidental, Lydia. I'm sure he knew."

"But how?"

"Same way I knew he had what I needed. Almost anyone can be bought, the hard part is figuring out the price."

"What did you need?"

"Ismae the Bloody."

Before

"**D**ID PRINCESS HAVE ANOTHER VISION?" BRITTANY mocks, letting herself be shoved into the men's bathroom of their borrowed campground.

"Ssshhh!" Tomas hisses as the door slams behind them. "Keep your voice down."

"Drama queen much?" She rolls her eyes and crosses her arms over her chest, leaning back against the wall. "She had another one of her little 'visions,' didn't she?" she demands.

"Yeah." Despite the intention as an accusation, Tomas finds himself agreeing, conflicted. He's known Brittany for the better part of a quarter of a century, and some of the others for longer. Still, when Zeke confided in him months ago he didn't go straight to her or them; he chose to keep Zeke's secret. *Her* secret.

"She's got you all wrapped around her little finger," she mutters.

"What're you talking about?"

Brittany sighs. "You, Zeke, the others. It's like she's some witch that cast a spell on all of you." Her voice drops to a sultry purr: "'Come, Tomas, follow me into fire . . . '" She moves her hips suggestively before tossing her head back in laughter.

"You're such a—"

"Ah-ah," Brittany scolds, wagging a finger at him. "You gonna hurl insults against your packsister over some singer with a few bad dreams and a worse voice?"

"It's not like that, Brit. You saw what happened last time."

"Sure!" she scoffs. "And I might be the only one. I saw a lucky guess. Maybe too lucky."

"What's that supposed to mean?"

"I mean do you *really* think Princess just woke up from a seizure with the whereabouts of this Keeper they dragged in for us to be hunting tonight? It's her first Hunt and her vision brings us the biggest prize of them all?"

"What're you getting at? That her visions are fake? That it's a power play by Zeke to elevate her status in the pack prematurely?"

"*Elevate? Prematurely?* Careful, T, the others hear you using such big words they'll expect more from you," she teases.

"Brit, I'm serious."

She shrugs. "Both, maybe. Maybe neither. I'm just sayin' that something's up. Why didn't any of our border packs catch this Keeper on his way in?"

"So they messed up. No one's perfect."

"You're right: no one's perfect."

"Yes. No one's perfect. That's what I said."

"*No* one's perfect," she repeats again for emphasis.

"You don't trust Zeke's judgment all of a sudden?"

"Not where she's concerned. Maybe she's playing him, too."

"She's your packmate, Brit. She went through the Rites just like you and me."

"And I'll have her back until she shows me I shouldn't—until then someone has to look out for the rest of you."

21

Now

TWO MEN LOGAN AND CHARLIE RECOGNIZE BUT cannot name lead them down halls they recognize but cannot place, towards a door neither have been through, into a yard they hardly remember. Charlie breathes deep the cool night air, feeling it expand her lungs for the first time since the night of her capture at Grady's property. She glances sideways at Logan who stares straight ahead at their handlers. She imagines him sizing them up, considering running just as she does—but that is not the plan and she is grateful it is logical Logan at her side rather than the hot-headed Hunter or curious Kiley.

She's never been good at remembering people's names, not because she doesn't want to.

"We're repairing the fence out here," the man with black, curly hair that reaches his chin barks over his shoulder.

"Wasn't Victor going to come?" Logan asks.

"You're a nosy one," the other man accuses.

"He's just nervous because you're vampires," Charlie interjects, infusing her words with more confidence than she feels, her tone flippant.

"Aren't you?" the black-haired man asks.

"No," she replies with a toss of her hair.

"He's busy with a visitor," he explains. "Don't worry though, we're under strict orders not to eat you," the man adds, but Charlie can hear the smile haunting his hollow reassurance.

"Don't push it though. I haven't had a bite in weeks," his comrade warns. Even in the dark Charlie notices about half of his right ear missing. What remains of it looks as though it were cut a little jagged, torn by teeth, maybe; a long section of flesh from his right ear up to the top of his head boasts just a few short, scraggly hairs jutting chaotically from thick gnarled scar tissue. He reminds her of a burn victim. "If we're missing the Hunt the least Victor could do is let us have a sip," he laments.

"The Hunt?" Charlie asks but neither man answers. She didn't expect them to.

The man stops them in front of the dilapidated fence.

"Can we just get this done? If you two behave, we'll let you stay out here with us after the work is done. Mess up and you won't see outside again. And if you run . . . "

"If you run, that gives us a reason to chase," the second man smiles, his fangs sliding forward and punctuating the threat.

Charlie and Logan murmur something that sounds like obedience.

"You two help Ray clear away the debris and—"

"Actually," Charlie interrupts, "I know how to use a circular saw to cut boards. I'm fast at it, too."

The man narrows his eyes, thinking.

"Charlie, we should stay together," Logan implores with furrowed brow.

"Relax, Logan. He already said that if we don't try anything stupid we're safe," she reassures him in a whisper loud enough she knows the men can hear.

"And you?" he asks Logan. "Can you work a saw?"

Logan shakes his head.

"Fine," the black-haired man says to Charlie. "You're with me then."

Logan catches her eye, hesitating before Ray nudges him, hard, between the shoulder blades with his elbow. He winces. She flashes him a quick smile and wave before bouncing after the scarred man.

◦◦◦

"You guys got a nice workbench," Charlie says, gravitating to the pile of boards next to the circular saw. She eyes the rows of tools on the pegboard wall, the orange and silver toolboxes scattered to create different workstations. "I love working outside, with my hands. Maybe if this goes well, you'll put in a good word with Victor?"

Then she spots it: two small takedown bows, strung, not ideal, but not ineffective. In the only unused corner of the large shed, a tarp folded up, waiting; practice arrows alight with neon green and orange paint; a half-rotted wood target, the paint well-worn. A lower-powered rifle, half-empty boxes of ammo strewn on the workbench on the next wall. Probably for scaring off coyotes when this was a working ranch, she figures, however long ago that might've been. Her gaze doesn't linger, though.

"Hey, is that a—" she starts, pointing at a Garden Weasel on the next wall.

"Look, I'm not into the small talk, so keep your mouth shut and make me some boards this long," he barks, pointing at the prototype.

"You know, this isn't the ideal length for the boards if you're trying to keep larger livestock in," she chatters away. "My dad used to say—"

He shakes his head and cuts her off. "I'm gonna see if pretty boy's ever even used a post-holer before."

Once he's outside, she begins rummaging as quietly as she can through the various tool chests, half her attention on the door. She pockets two Swiss Army knives she finds before she hears the crunch of footstep-on-threshold as her hands reappear from her hoodie pockets to rest empty on the top of the tool chest. She runs her hand along the metal.

"What're you doing?" the black-haired man demands.

"Looking for the brackets you're using—you're using new ones, right? Not the ones from last season?"

"Get back to the saw, kid—or it's back inside to rot. And yeah, we are. They're over there." He points towards the workbench nearest the saw.

She shrugs and starts feeding boards through, humming to herself.

"Shoot!" she cries, a board clattering to the ground. "Well that's not salvageable," she mutters, holding up the too-short board, aware from her peripheral vision that the black-haired man heard her. She begins humming again.

"What're you doing?" he asks, crossing to stand over her.

She pauses to show him. "It's that board I wrecked. Just sawing it down into kindling. Once it dries out it won't go to waste."

"Whatever makes you happy, kid," he mutters, stepping again outside when he hears a crash and Logan cussing loudly.

Charlie takes up a few of the pieces of kindling, slipping them underneath her hooded sweatshirt and T-shirt, and tucking them underneath a belt she fastened tightly around her bustline. She winces as she feels splinters of newly sawn wood jab into her skin but she tucks as many as she can without appearing bulky.

She hears his footsteps before he gets near enough to matter, her eyes lingering over the mounted bows, the last thing she sees before she turns, greeting him.

"So . . . has he?"

"Has who what?" the black-haired man asks, busying himself with something across the toolshed.

"Has Logan ever used a post-holer?"

Now

"**I** THOUGHT YOU'D NEVER GET BACK,**"** KILEY POUTS, bounding out of bed to greet her friends at the door. "How was it?"

"It was nice to be outside again," Logan offers, casting a look after the man who'd already turned, grumbling about being hungry after all that work.

The small talk continues amongst them until the door seals shut and for several seconds after. Then Charlie and Logan lead the other two into the bathroom, each bending down, tugging up on their pants legs and fiddling with something. Thick sticks and wooden post fragments clatter to the tile floor. Charlie then tosses two Swiss Army knives onto the pile.

"Let's get 'em pointy," she jokes.

"In here," Hunter suggests. "That way we can hide everything and flush the shavings."

"That'll clog it," Kiley points out.

"With any luck we won't be here long enough for that to matter," Logan states rather solemnly.

The others nod.

"Put the shavings into plastic bags and hide the plastic bags where housekeeping won't find them," Kiley suggests.

"Or into the kitchen trash. I doubt they dig in there," Logan points out.

"Shouldn't be much shavings anyway, so Logan's right," says Charlie. "You guys work on the tips. I'm going to carve notches in all of them and add counterweight."

"Notches?" Hunter asks.

"Didn't I mention?" Charlie grins.

She unzips her hooded sweatshirt to reveal two

takedown bows, taken down and disassembled beyond even what the manufacturer intended, each secured to her torso by a thick braided leather belt under her bustline, one in front, one in back, the lower ends secured in the waistband of her jeans. The other three stand stunned, slack-jawed. "You wanted weapons."

"How did you . . . " Logan starts to ask.

"Turns out I'm not only a bit stronger," she brags. "I'm also a bit faster. Strapped 'em to me right before we headed inside."

"That's why that guy asked why you were walking funny. You didn't really drop a post-holer on your foot, did you?" Logan asks, referencing their being herded back inside.

She shrugs. "I think they were ready to cut us loose and explain it to Victor later, for as much as I annoyed them."

"*That's* why that one guy kept coming out to bother us!" Logan laughs, clapping Charlie on the back. "Also, you're a terrible singer. If Taylor Swift were dead, she'd be rolling in her grave."

"Darn right I am!" she jokes before launching into a few bars of "Shake It Off," making Hunter cringe.

"This is really happening," Kiley mutters underneath the mirth, taking a seat on the floor in front of the toilet.

"Stay with us," Charlie encourages as she loosens the belt, noticing the glisten of a thin sheen of sweat broken out over Kiley's forehead. "It's a good plan— and quite possibly the best timing for it."

"You think we'll have enough?" Hunter asks, surveying the pile of debris as he takes the bows from Charlie.

"If we need more, we can take apart a chair. And remember, if the shaft isn't broken and you have time, pull the arrow out of the animal. They're reus—" but she's interrupted by the sound of wretching and the splash of wet-on-wet.

Logan drops to his knees next to Kiley, gathering her hair and pulling it off her neck and out of the splash zone. He looks to Charlie and Hunter who take the hint, moving towards the door with a slight nod each.

"Logan to the res—" Hunter begins but Charlie elbows him, hard, in the ribs.

"Not the time," she warns, pulling the door shut behind them to give Logan and Kiley some privacy.

23

Now

"DID YOU SERIOUSLY JUST *PUSH* ME, BRO?"

From under the bed, Charlie watches Logan step towards Hunter, his chest puffed out. She eyes Kiley who leans back against the headboard of her bed, legs stretched out, crossed at the ankles in front of her, flipping through a copy of *Popular Science* Victor had finished with and passed along to her.

"Did you seriously just say 'bro'?" Kiley mocks from behind the magazine she pretends to read.

Hunter laughs. "Even your girlfriend thinks you're a moron. It's okay, dude, we shouldn't have trusted the jock to be able to read—" but he doesn't get to finish his taunt before Logan lunges, knocking him down to the ground with a grunt.

Kiley shrieks and tosses the magazine onto the comforter. "Stop!" She jumps ups from her bed, helpless to stop the fray that ensues, edging nearer them but far enough away to not get mistaken for a target.

Charlie hears the shower running from behind the closed bathroom door in between the two boys' grunts and Kiley's louder-than-necessary shrieking. The boys crash into the table and chairs, one of the chairs splintering under the weight of a shoved Logan. Hunter leaps onto him, drawing back a fist, cocked and ready.

Finally the doors to the suite slide open, the two men from her and Logan's yard shift the night before rushing in. They scan the room: Kiley shrieking, the two boys crashing, the closed bathroom door from behind which Charlie is sure they hear the shower running—after all, she can. Satisfied, they waste no time crossing the room and diving into the fray. As she slithers on her stomach out from under the bed and darts out into the empty hall, she silently hopes the two men don't rough up her co-captives too badly.

But she can't think about that. She pulls from her back pocket the rumpled map Hunter drew from memory that would lead her to the electrical room, the central nerve hub of at least this section of the grounds, though surely not the only. Inside she wasn't sure what she'd find: that wasn't a part of Hunter's tour with Victor while she lay in the infirmary, tubes pumping *their* blood into her, righting their wrong, keeping her more alive than either of their kind.

She doesn't have time to overthink his scratchy notes, barely legible. The boys' diversion will only buy her a few minutes, but she's armed with a reason to be out of the suite and looking so frantic.

She hears the low thrum of the facility's veins before she sees the door. Lucky for her Hunter was right: instead of being secured in the fashion typical of the rest of the facility—at least, the rest he'd seen—this room relied on keyed entry just in case the electrical system failed or backfired or was somehow hacked and someone needed to cut the power. She took a bobby pin from her hair and wiggled it in the lock, back and forth a few times, then jabbed it deeper into the keyhole.

Click.

Her father's gun cabinet locked mostly for show, she'd learned this trick when too young to be fingering the smooth walnut and maple and birch stocks, the cold steel barrels—but sometimes when she had a nightmare nothing else would make her feel safe, so she'd sneak into his den and pick the lock. One time he caught her. She burst into tears, laying the heavy rifle beside her on the floor. He crouched down next to her, wiped away a trickle of tears, and said, "Let me show you where I keep the key, but don't let your mother catch you." And she never did.

She glances around before she slips inside, confirming what she knows, that no one's followed her. The click of the door behind her. She faces the shiny and sleek of metal casing, lights dancing on the facility's UPS. This Uninterruptable Power System takes over every other night when the main grid powers down, according to Hunter's notes, ensuring seamless running of all of the facility's core functions.

Seamless running, like clockwork, but not tonight. Tonight the main grid will go down, and the door to the suite—and all the doors between them and the outside, along with all the security cameras, scanners, lights, all of it—will go still as these precious dark minutes tick by.

What Hunter's notes fail to account for, of course: a lithium-ion battery UPS rather than an electric or gas generator and she hadn't thought to ask if he actually *heard* the generator from outside the door. Charlie runs her hand just barely over the wires, thick and thin, green and red and yellow and black and gray. The plan was to disable the UPS so that when the main grid powers down it does not immediately kick on—but she sees the series of tubes that maintain the liquid-cooled system and the temperature sensor.

She doesn't have time to overthink it. She'll

explain it later to the others, amend the plan from there. She pulls a pair of pliers from her back jeans pocket and a few deft movements later finishes what she came to do. She drops the pliers to the floor and kicks them underneath the UPS, then listens to the thrum of the chaos to come, which only she can hear. Papa always stored the ammo separate from the guns and high up; but here she had all she needed.

In the hall she hears the commotion from their suite continue, except that Kiley's shrieks come at longer intervals and no longer with exaggerated volume. Footsteps between her and them, but she doesn't stop, rounding a corner in a sprint.

"Whoa!" Victor catches her by the shoulders.

"Victor! The guys—they were fighting and-and the security guys—the redhead and the other one from the yard," she stalls with the unnecessary detail. " . . . I'm afraid they're going to hurt them!" Charlie manages between quick breaths. "I was looking for you, come on!"

She grabs him by the arm and runs for the suite, doors still open. They're greeted by the men from the yard dragging a bloodied Logan and a bloodied Hunter by the collars. The redhead tosses Logan at Victor's feet.

"Fighting over a girl!"

"Where'd she—" the other starts, looking at Charlie.

"*He* was," Hunter, black-eye blooming, interjects loudly, spitting at Logan but missing.

"Was not . . . " Logan grumbles, wiping blood from his lip, glaring up at Hunter.

"I'll take it from here, gentlemen," Victor says, dismissing the other two vampires who smirk.

"Little snake bit me!" one tells the other as they start down the hall. "Had half a mind to bite him back."

"Guys," Victor barks, helping Logan to his feet. "I know you're going a bit stir-crazy, but we've talked about this. You're lucky Charlie found me—you might've ended up a snack for those two. Now let me see—" He cups Hunter's chin but Hunter jerks his head away. Victor sighs. "Did the others get a few hits in?"

Logan and Hunter hesitate, then nod.

"Does it hurt?"

They nod again.

"Seems like they punished you enough. Don't let it happen again. Now let's go down to the infirmary so Doctor Larkin can clean you up. You might need a couple stitches in that lip," Victor warns before turning to give the girls at the entrance to the suite a quick wave as the door closes between them.

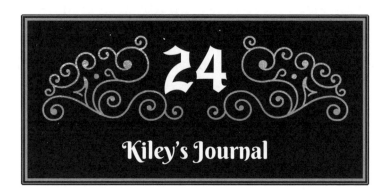

24

Kiley's Journal

SOMETHING'S CHANGING. VICTOR DIDN'T EVEN SCOLD the men who roughed up Logan and Hunter. I don't think the others noticed, but I did. He's preoccupied, which is both good and bad news for us: the more divided his attention, the less he's focusing on us—but the less he's focusing on us the less protection he offers.

The plan is a good one, I guess, but I'm worried. We only need one of us to escape but I'm afraid for whomever is left behind. I think maybe we've worn out our welcome.

25

Now

"I T'S GOING TO *EXPLODE*?!" KILEY WHISPER-YELLS AT Charlie, eyes wide.

"Sort of. Yes. Absolutely," Charlie stammers, brow crinkled. "It seemed like a good idea at the time."

"How?" Kiley challenges, Logan and Hunter joining her to stand opposite Charlie like the last line of defense in a battle they knew they already lost.

Charlie puts her hands on her hips and opens her mouth to speak but is interrupted.

"No, I mean 'How?' Like, '*How* could you? *How* could this seem like a good idea? *How* could you do this without talking to us first? We're all gonna die?!'"

Her voice rising to shrill, she hears Logan shush her so she responds with a glare in his direction.

"She's right. We didn't *agree* on exploding, Charlie. We *agreed* on escaping quietly, slipping out when the generator failed to take over and power the facility. We *all agreed* that our best shot out of here is to cause *quiet* confusion—that way they don't charge in here, fangs blazing, ready to drag us off to 'the tanks,' whatever those are," Hunter explains in too cool a tone from his clenched jaw, his fists balled at his sides, each trembling as if he himself might explode.

"I know that's what we decided—" she starts, hands up in front of her, gesturing 'calm down' or 'surrender,' it doesn't matter.

Hunter lunges forward and grabs her by the collar. "Yes, *we* decided—and then you *un*decided. If one of us dies it's on *you*."

"Cool it, man," Logan warns a few beats later than he normally would, as if unsure for a moment if he should stop Hunter from roughing up Charlie, or worse. Hunter lets go of her collar with a shove.

"Undo it," Kiley demands.

"Undo it?" Logan asks.

"Yeah, she got us into this, she can get us out."

"We can't risk leaving the suite again," he reasons.

"She can. She's fast and besides, if one of us dies it *should* be her."

"Kiley!"

"It can't be undone," Charlie states. "It *will* explode. You can either hang out here when that happens and hope they're not so pissed that they slaughter any of us they find, or you can use this as a chance to get home."

"Won't it look like an accident?" Logan asks. "They might not think it's us."

"Sure, it could. But us making a break for it won't and I'm not spending a single second here that I don't have to."

"No way, me either," Hunter agrees.

"The explosion isn't going to bring the facility

down, but it'll do some serious damage to their operations if they don't have enough power to sustain it," Charlie explains, grateful for Hunter's support, no matter how fleeting.

"How do you know that?"

"When people aren't sure you're going to live they run their mouths around you. I wasn't conscious but I was *aware*."

She steps towards Kiley, nose-to-nose. "People are gonna die, Kiley—it's your choice if you're one of them or not."

Cold, perhaps—but not colder than Kiley telling her she should be the one to die. Charlie pushes past the three, out of the bathroom and into the main room of the suite. With nowhere else to go and nothing to do but wait, she lies on her bed, puts in earbuds and closes her eyes to seethe in relative peace.

She could tell Kiley that they might die. She could tell her some of the vampires might even die. The truth that she swallows for all their sakes is that the majority of who might die are just people—like them, but hooked up to some tanks somewhere, helpless as their blood is siphoned—and they didn't get to add their voices to the plan.

26

Now

SOMEWHERE: THE HISS OF THICK CHEMICAL MELTING what's in its path. Metal, wires, plastic. Putrid sludge creeping over the mess of mechanical innards, devouring.

Elsewhere: a rumble, a flicker.

They all sit on the bed nearest the door, waiting. Each outfitted with sharpened fragments of wood, two with takedown bows and crude arrows, all secured with twine, elastic from waistbands, belts, whatever they could find. One taps a foot, his arm around the one who bites her lip as tears stream down her cheeks. One stares ahead, concentrating on the swelling silence as it fills the room. One fidgets with her hair.

"When?" the tearful one says.

"Soon." Another fidgets.

A few moments pass: "When?" Tap, tap, tap.

"I don't know." Tug, tug, fidget.

"How can you not know?" Wipes trails of wet from her cheeks.

"I've never done this before." Twirling her ponytail into a bun.

"You've never done this before?" Tap, tap, tap.

"When would I have done this before?" Lets her ponytail fall.

"Can we all just be quiet, please?" Still staring.

A few moments pass: "Is everyone ready?" Tug, tug.

Mumble, mumble.

"Everyone's good on the plan?" Flips her ponytail over her shoulder again.

Nodding.

Only one of them hears the rumble, feels it in her bones, but everyone notices the flicker of the overhead lights, like every hallway in every hospital in every bad zombie movie's first few frames. Flickering turns to a blackness that swallows even the alarm clock's glow, the tiny red and green and yellow lights around the video screen by the door, the soft gray light of the screen itself.

The earlier silence rings so loud in memory as true silence settles in to contradict it, thick. No humming of the lights, no knocking of the refrigerator, no high-pitch buzz of the security monitors; all the sounds you don't hear because they've become a part of you, snuffed out. The pressure of nothing building in your ear just before the ringing starts, as if uncomfortable in the silence.

Faces look to one another in the darkness.

Whispers.

"Is that it?"

"I don't think so?"

"Should we run?"

"I don't hear anything in the hall."

But timing is funny that way as a low rumble freight-trains through the halls and echoes in all eight of their ears, through all eight hundred and twenty-four of their bones.

"Now!"

Four bodies that didn't anticipate the density of darkness scramble for a door three of them cannot see, one slightly ahead of the rest. She pries open the sliding door with a grunt, bloodying a nailbed as the nail tears from it but she doesn't notice. Two hands grope for one another and clasp behind her; the third body offering the fourth her stake to grab instead. Someone pokes her hand with something and she recoils for just a beat before clasping the stake and dragging the chain of captives behind her—lead by a bow, the same guarding the rear.

The hall: just as dark towards freedom, illuminated by a soft flickering orange in the direction of the oversized mechanical closet. The hall: silent ahead, towards the uncertainty of freedom; voices behind, towards the safety of captivity. Still time to change their minds but their resolve weathers this pause. *Tss-tss-tss-tss* of sprinklers as they rain overhead. The leader pulls them deeper into the ink that seems to swallow them all.

Rounding a few corners, a doorway now yawns open at the end of this hall, casting a faint light into the corridor. The captives stop short, a collective gasp. Hands unclasp from hands, from one another's weapons to focus on their own. One gestures for them to continue, her pace quickening. They each hold their breath as they creep past the room with the light.

Empty. Exhale in relief.

Another turn and darkness ahead. Though three of them can't see it, they know that this hall ends in a door and beyond that, moonlight and dew-soaked grass and the fresh air of wide-open and pinpoints of starlight. Kiley and Hunter push forward, starved for it.

Footsteps behind them, but only the part of

Charlie that is more than human hears. She draws her bow and nocks an arrow, but instead of the interloper she sees Grady in his truck barreling at the men who came for her. She sees the man she shot in the head stand back up. She sees the too-bright fluorescent lighting in the too-clean infirmary as she woke up, alone, a tube filling her veins with *their* blood.

I'm not going back, she thinks as she lets the arrow fly.

Now

WHAT CAUSES DELILAH TO DOUBLE OVER AND FALL to her knees isn't the arrow lodged so near her still heart, nor the explosion that erupts behind her through a labyrinth of fluorescently-lit corridors. No, the explosion itself, which causes the four captives to crouch and cover their ears, doesn't penetrate the barrage of images flooding the part of her brain where memories sometimes shake loose.

She's got a hole in her. We'll lose points for that.

The scratch of hay on her arms, her abdomen where once a blessed bullet tore into her and burned. Except that this flesh scratched by hay is not hers, was never shot by a blessed bullet. A spurt of red from the head of a man too far away to see well but she can anyway. Headlights and truck. A dead man walks. Flames, a winding country road, the buzz of crickets. The long-short-long et cetera of Morse code but she doesn't know what it spells. Something about mending a fence, learning to shoot. Annie Oakley.

Memories that aren't hers.

I'm not going back. I'm not going back. I'm not going back.

Delilah looks to the blond girl who just shot her as she recovers from crouching to nock another arrow.

Wait. Delilah puts her hands in front of her and slowly stands. She cares little if the girl shoots again, the crude arrows unlikely to find their mark; she cares that she can hear the girl's thoughts somehow, but even that question falls behind why these kids are even here. Then she remembers: Lydia's pack, Morgeaux, Quinn. They may have toyed with the girl but bringing her with them—bringing her *here*—was their objective. But why?

What the—? Charlie shakes her head, perhaps she imagined the woman's plea? She draws back the bowstring.

I can help you.

Charlie pauses. *Stop it! Get out of my head!*

I don't know what's going on here but I helped another girl get away. The front door leads to the yard which has Praedari scrambling to figure out what's going on—we need to find another way out.

You're one of them, Charlie silently accuses.

No, I'm a Keeper. We're at war. I shouldn't be here. Neither should you.

Charlie gives the woman a single head-bob, but not before looking between the other captives, each rising to stand again, shaking their heads to try and clear the ringing, and this woman. There's no way that she alone could get these three to safety and she knows it. If they were all like her, maybe, but the truth she found herself unwilling to acknowledge until now is that she only ever needed one of them to make it out alive—and that was probably going to be her.

28

Now

EANWHILE, IN THE YARD:

"Why're we even doing this?" Liam asks, punctuating his question with a grunt as he lifts the marble tomb cut to the precise size of the one who rests within.

"Victor spoke hastily. That Keeper may mean something to him, but we mean more—he just needs to find himself again. Until then, we act with honor and support the sect—which means this place and its alpha."

"Mina . . . " Liam starts as his sister hoists her end of the enclosure.

"Yes, Liam?"

"Let's just say he doesn't realize his mistake and he follows through with it. I need you to let me be the one to die." A statement, his voice does not waver.

"And your sacrifice would be an honorable death—but I cannot let you. The future of our family rests in your Blood and your blood, brother. It is not your time."

"No, it's my fault we have to make this choice," he asserts, brow furrowing. "If only I'd tried harder to talk you out of it . . ."

"Liam, the All-Father himself couldn't have changed my mind, nor would I want it changed," she explains, the softness of her tone disarming her brother.

"The All-Father?" Liam forces a chuckle. "You think you'd be offered a place in Valhalla, dear sister? I've bested you in more shield-bashing bouts than I could count."

"Liam, I'm serious. Freyja blessed you and your wife with a son, and his son with sons and daughters, and they need you to Usher them when they come of age."

Liam starts to speak but Mina releases one hand from underneath her end of the tomb to cut him off. She dips with the weight of the marble for a beat before two hands once again support it.

"Freyja may not have chosen me for motherhood, but I love your line as my own."

With this how could he argue? His sisters had seen their nephew born, had wiped sweat from his wife's brow with a cool damp rag, had held her in their arms as she pushed him into this world, a pink thing mewling and squalling. Mina and Quinn had wiped the baby down and led him through the Blessing Rite before handing him to Liam, their touch and voice known to his son before his own. Mina loved her niece and nephew, Quinn's children. But it was Liam's Eirik who stole her heart, and in his children and his children's children the future of their Blood.

He eyes his sister a moment before changing the subject. "Should we be as alarmed as the others about the generator malfunction?" he asks, glancing nearer the house where shadows dart around, their fellow Praedari scrambling to discern the source of the explosion, if it could really be called such—no louder than mortars, at least out here on the property.

"It's probably as simple as a circuit shorting or something overheating. I'm not sure how it impacts the operation, though. As far as I know, Victor just wanted us to move her to somewhere far enough from the chaos so she's unlikely to be endangered by things like this in the future—or, you know, if we come under siege by the Keepers."

"So, a storm cellar? How is that more secure? Those kids could probably pry the doors open, let alone other Everlasting."

Mina shrugs in response. "Secure from what? Nearly everyone here is too afraid of her to come any nearer than required. The kids stay in their suite and wouldn't know a sleeping Elder from a corpse. And *she's* not going anywhere of her own volition any time soon."

"What about the Keeper?"

"Either she has no idea that we have Ismae the Bloody or that's exactly why she's here." She shrugs. "I say we wake up Ismae and let the Keeper take her chances. We have the kids, what is Victor waiting for?"

Now

"THERE'S TOO MUCH ACTIVITY IN THE FRONT YARD," I whisper, the four teens crowding behind me, four heartbeats crashing in four sternums. "We need to find another way out."

"Hunter!" Charlie exclaims in a whisper.

"Yeah? Oh, well, I—" he stammers, raking his hand through his hair.

"Did you see anything on your tour? A back door or a basement or maybe a big window that opens?" Charlie suggests.

"We don't have Kiley's notebook with our notes . . . " he starts to explain.

"So? You have a photographic memory, right?"

"*Eidetic* memory—and, well, no," Hunter manages.

"What?"

"I lied. Well, I exaggerated. It doesn't *really* exist. I mean, they've only found it in children, not—"

"You *what*?" Charlie interrupts, not bothering to whisper.

"We don't have time for this, just follow me," I bark.

I've been here before, that much I know. I just need something to shake loose a memory, a flash of who I was before I can't remember, before my Becoming. I scan the darkness for familiar wood paneling, running my hand along it as we creep through the gutted ranch house, carpet pulled up and out to reveal hardwood that doesn't match the paneling, rooms no longer where they once were as if only skeleton remains of this place. Of course, those walls where once probably hung photos or small shelves with thimbles or souvenir spoons or other knickknacks find themselves bare. A few spots boast brighter pigmentation to the wood, a reverse shadow effect where sun faded around something hanging.

Then I spot it.

იო

"You're *sure* your mom will like this?" I ask, setting the light purple, rose-patterned gift bag embossed with a gold foil "Happy Birthday!" on the breakfast bar.

"Positive," Victor reassures as he steps forward and wraps his arms around my waist.

"She's going to know you picked it," I challenge, glancing to the gift.

He shrugs. "You know she likes you, she always has. You've known each other for over ten years. It's not like this is the first time you're meeting her."

"She likes me as your friend, not as your girlfriend."

"She *likes* you—regardless what you are to me."

"'If you climb in the saddle be ready for the ride!'?" I scrunch my face into a grimace at the words on the gift.

"It's a thing people say out here!" he defends. "They've really embraced this western lifestyle."

My eyes follow where he gestures. Pairs of cowboy boots in varying shades of earth and jewel tones lined up as if in a museum, mud and dust either cleaned from them or never sullied them.

"I mean, it's cute, I guess, but is it appropriate for my boyfriend's *mother*?"

"You know what? I'm no longer interested in hearing you doubt how amazing you are . . . " he says softly, putting his fingers to my lips to shush me.

Then he leans in, his lips just meeting mine. "They won't be here until tomorrow," he whispers, the shape of each word traced onto my lips by his. Goosebumps break out over my arms, legs, back, chest. I inhale his scent, his usual cologne emphasized by sweat and pine pitch from doing chores.

The memory fades as quickly as it comes on, leaving my body with a shudder. Still hanging where the living room once arched into the kitchen, the sage green-and-cream cross-stitch I gave his mother, Lanita, the first time Victor brought me to a family gathering as his girlfriend. I snatch it off the wall, grounding myself partially in the landscape of the brain where memory dwells, a trick I learned when I needed to explore a vision for just a few seconds longer. Though, not a vision: this has already happened. Somehow the truth of it feels so much further away.

But it's enough.

I lead the captives through fossils of rooms preserved only in memory—no more closets, very few windows, once-doorways now without hinge or knob. From one such doorway I see the monolith of a stone fireplace dividing the old living room, which marks that I'm on the right path; beyond it, the glass sliding doors to the patio, now darkly-tinted.

Through it I do not see movement, only moonlight and, in the distance, mountains. I step outside, slabs of light stone underfoot, chiseled to look haphazard though they fit together like puzzle pieces. A pergola overhead, burnt-out twinkle lights woven among the beams. Beyond them, stars.

"Delilah!" a voice calls out as the body it inhabits rounds the corner.

The five of us freeze.

"Victor!" I feign a smile and take a few steps towards him to head him off before he reaches the patio door.

Don't move! I mentally shout, hoping the blond girl can hear me. *The glass is dark enough he may not see you. Don't make a sound.*

No response.

"What's going on?"

"Just a malfunction in the ol' engine room," he says with a tight-lipped smile. "Ships like this don't always sail smooth. You really shouldn't be out here, though," he warns.

"I know, but the power went out and I thought I should find you and see if I could help rather than sit in the dark alone and useless," I lie with a grin that I'm sure is too plastered on.

"Well I'm just heading back inside to check our status," he explains, taking a few steps towards me, now in front of the half of the patio door that is still closed. "Here," he says, placing his hand on the small of my back and pressing firmly. "I'll take you back to your suite."

"It's really not necessary," I argue, but he guides me the few steps to the open door anyway.

I move so that my body takes up as much empty space in the doorframe as it can, turning towards him. I lean in, looking up at him. He leans in, too, his body mirroring mine. I wrap my arms around him, ignoring the tingle of desire as it blooms in my lower spine and coils upwards like hitting the fast-forward button on ivy growing up a trellis.

"You never were the helpless one, were you?" he asks, his finger tracing from my shoulder up my neck, stopping at the nape where his palm outstretches, his fingers lacing through my dark curls. His lips don't quite brush mine when a loud crash from inside startles me, the predator within me jolting to attention as I turn my head towards the distraction and snarl.

His beast-self rises to meet mine, perhaps, or is likewise startled to vigilance. He shoves me aside and rushes to fill the space between the cause and me, fists clenched. Stunned, I keep pressed against the frame of the still-closed patio door, feet straddling the threshold, the metal pressing into my back and skull. I could run. I could run and there's a chance no one would catch me, a chance he wouldn't chase me.

My own beast's jaw snaps as she growls within me, ready for a fight for my sake or the captives'—or to sate her own hunger—I'm not sure. I haven't allowed my gaze to follow Victor's, too sure of what I'll find: four shaking, wide-eyed teenagers and a pile of broken glass or knocked-down books or a horizontal lamp—oh, it doesn't matter what they did to cause the crash that unleashed Victor's attention upon them, does it? I open my mouth to intervene but when I look to them my jaw drops: where once four stood, only two remain. And they're already making the mess worse.

"W—we were j—just . . . " one starts, scratching his head before grunting and then laughing uneasily.

"He means we heard—" the girl who nudged the boy in the ribs interrupts.

"Save it," Victor snaps, turning to address me, lips pursed. "And you?"

My eyes dart from the two kids who dare not move to Victor's accusing gaze. Then the ground swells, pitching me forward.

ৡৎ

Where once the four teenagers stood, they now lie sleeping, tubes like IVs in each of their arms. Their chests rise and fall with the slow cadence of slumber. I crawl on all fours, following the tubes like a trail for what seems like forever, funhouse mirror-style, to find that they converge and feed into a thicker tube connected to a woman. She sleeps like the four teenagers but with the thick tube down her throat rather than in her arms like IVs. Bound at the wrists and ankles, her chest does not rise and fall like theirs. She feels familiar. I want to touch her. I reach out and stroke the cool marble encasement instead and I think of Snow White. Then of the poison apple.

Time passes, but only here. So much time spins by in mere seconds.

Her eyes open.

I can feel her hunger. Our hunger. The hunger of decades—no, of centuries. A hunger only an army could quench, if it could indeed be quenched. A hunger I've at once never felt before and know intimately.

Come closer, Childe, and I glance around us. I know that beyond these sleeping four the two real teenagers stand huddled, bathed in moonlight, trembling. Here they look so peaceful—not the desperate, dreamless death-sleep of the Everlasting but genuine sleep, full of possibility. Their only hope for escape until tonight.

Who are you? Why are you here? Where are we? My lips form the words that follow voicelessly.

You'll know soon enough. With any luck, only after it's too late, I hear a woman's voice but again her lips do not move.

You are one of them?

It will make sense in time. Though it be not your nature, I need you to be patient and trust me. I need you to stand down. You know not what you're meddling with.

❧

"Delilah?"

The haze of the vision clears and I am on my back staring up into Victor's gray eyes, his expression unreadable.

Hello? Hello? But no one answers—neither the

woman who spoke to me in my vision, nor the blond girl who's disappeared.

"Delilah, what's going on? Why did I find you prowling around the patio with them?" Victor asks, eyes narrowed, studying me.

Still, he helps me to sit up, swallowing his hesitance. I look between the kids and Victor and back, my eyes resting on them.

I'm sorry. But with the blond girl gone I know only I hear my apology.

"I was coming to find you, like I said," I start, returning my gaze to him. " . . . because I found them trying to escape. They were armed and—"

I'm sorry. I'm sorry.

And dear reader, I was.

Before

"**I** CAN'T BELIEVE ZEKE LET YOU OUT OF HIS SIGHT, especially tonight," Tomas grins as we come up on the junkyard and storage facility purported to be from the vision I feigned earlier. He clutches a metal pipe in one hand, letting it bang against the chain-link fence we hopped to get inside.

"*Let* me?" I challenge, biting back a smile. I put my hand on my hip which I jut out for emphasis.

I don't bother to whisper, my lack of caution mirroring Tomas's. I know where our quarry hides, one of the more dilapidated cement-and-steel-beamed warehouses on the outer edge of the facility scouted for exactly this purpose months ago by me and Zeke. I find myself grateful for Tomas, his crude banter giving me something to focus on besides the Hunt.

"I thought he'd want to celebrate all up close and personal-like," he says, voice lower. He steps towards me and reaches out to brush my hair from my shoulder. "A victory lap on a pile of Keeper ashes. Maybe a celebratory kiss? How romantic would that be?"

I roll my eyes. "You've got a skewed sense of what's romantic, Tomas."

He fakes a frown. "I'm just sayin' he keeps a tight leash on you," he explains.

"Or maybe *he's* the one on the leash," Brittany interjects as she drops down next to us onto all fours from the top of the fence where she kept watch.

"Oh good. *There* you are," I snap.

She stands. "I'm a Praedari and this is my pack. Of course I'm here. Besides, not all of us have a sugar daddy for an Usher—some of us have to earn our keep. Some of us haven't missed a Howling since our Becoming."

"Sure, this is your pack—until a better one comes along," I prod.

A modern traditionalist, if there were such a thing, she derives a sense of superiority from following the traditions of the Praedari to the letter—at least, to the letter as she learned them from her previous pack, and the pack before that, and the pack before that. To her face they refer to her as a survivor. Behind her back, less flattering things. Still, her loyalty rivals that of Tomas.

"Who knew Brittany'd be a stickler for attendance records," Tomas teases, attempting to diffuse the situation. "You keeping our report cards, too?"

"It seems like you have something to say to me," I demand, stepping towards her. "Or maybe you want to take a swing?"

She steps towards me in response. "If it weren't a sacred night I'd take a bite, you little—"

"Ladies, ladies—there's enough of me to go around," Tomas says as he steps between us, his attempt at lightening the mood transparent.

"Back off, Tomas. I'm warning you," she growls.

"Come on. We should find the others." I try to sneak a glance at my watch but Brittany catches me.

"Got somewhere to be?" Brittany challenges.

I pick up a brick and toss it between my hands, not breaking eye contact with her.

"*We* do, actually. Or have you forgotten we're *hunting* right now?"

I turn away from the two and scan the landscape. The smell of rotting earth and motor oil thick in my nostrils, I point to the row of neglected, over-sized shipping containers at the edge of the junkyard between us and what will become ground zero in precisely twenty-two minutes.

In twenty-two minutes the operative whose cover was blown will lead the Praedari pursuing him here. As their quarry for this sacred hunt, they give him an hour head start, though border packs usually won't let the hunted out of the territory, instead making it into a game of cat-and-mouse. It's usually a border pack that gets the kill as the hunted tries to flee rather than find a place from which to fight. In twenty-two minutes I'm to make sure my marks follow me to the rendezvous, as Zeke's will follow him—*rendezvous*, a misnomer, in a way: yes, we are to meet there, but me and Zeke will be the only two to leave. In twenty-two minutes: the beginning of the end.

We weave in and out of the shipping containers, making quick work of our search. The full moon illuminates more than we need, so much wasted light. Movement in the distance catches my eye so I signal to Brittany and Tomas to follow, but I don't wait.

Within a minute or so Tomas catches up to me.

"Where's Brittany?"

He shrugs. "She'll catch up, right?"

"Yeah," I start. "I heard something over there and thought we'd go in together. You know, get the kill as a pack, bond or whatever." I resist the urge to check my watch, not wanting to draw attention to my hyper-vigilance.

"Delilah, she'll come around. Don't waste too

much energy forcing it. Come on!" he encourages, clapping me on the back.

"Wait!" I say, grabbing him by the arm. "I mean, will she? Are you sure?" I ask, crinkling my brow in concern.

"Does it matter?" He shrugs again. "Where is this coming from?"

"I've just been thinking. A lot of what she's said is right. Do the others feel that way?" I look at my hand still holding his arm and force the Blood to my cheeks. As my skin warms with flush, I look away and let my hand drop.

He steps closer. "Look, I've known you longer than you've known you," he starts, my jaw dropping slightly in consideration of protest. He holds up a hand to stop me. "Zeke told me about how you don't remember anything before your Becoming. But me and him, we knew you. Maybe not *well*, but you can learn a lot about someone while listening to them sing their hearts out night after night." He bites back a grin. I feel the pink in my cheeks darken to crimson and for a moment I'm unsure whether it's the Blood or genuine.

He leans in and for a moment I think he might kiss me. "She's not forever. You are." He tucks a rogue curl behind my ear and kisses my forehead as a brother might. "Now, let's find us a Keeper to suck dry!"

He whoops as we make our way to the dilapidated concrete building, an old warehouse that stored who-knows-what at the edge of the property line, as if to conjure up from some depth the Tomas I know: reckless and antagonistic, overconfident by miles. Barbed wire coils along the top of the chain-link fence here, rusted. The corpse of something too far gone to identify rots near the door I know to be the only door we can pry open, the sharp tang of decay overwhelming my sense of smell. Moonlight casts a sliver onto the dirt floor inside through the gap that tells me someone else has pried this door open and spent the time to push it closed again.

Zeke.

Tomas and I silently pry the door open, communicating by head nods and pointing and a series of crude hand signals our pack has come to rely on over the years, some starting as a joke and sticking. I lead us into the wide-open space of the main floor, scan the room as if I'm here for the first time. Two wide metal staircases lead up to a mostly obscured partial second floor and repeat themselves for two floors after. From there, three narrow metal staircases lead further up, into the rafter beams, a sort of makeshift catwalk.

I gesture to the staircase nearest us and he leads. We hear rustling and movement above. I glance between Tomas ascending the stairs and the door we came in, anticipating Brittany's arrival. We've neared the top of the stairs when we hear a slam followed by shouting and the thundering of a few sets of feet running on the metal, grate-style flooring of a partial level above us. Tomas is already running to follow when I hear a noise at the front entrance. I turn in time to see the darkening of the main room as the moonlight withdraws. Someone's closed off my escape route. I glance at my watch and feel my dead heart wither further into my ribcage.

It starts as a rumble, like a large power grid working just a bit harder to keep up with the demands placed on it except this place hasn't seen electricity in years. Bare wires hang, no longer connected to anything.

There's a second rumble, louder than the first. With Tomas at least a floor above me, I turn and run down the stairs, not caring who might hear the clanging of my boots on the metal. The door is too heavy for me to pry open alone, so I run for the other side of the main floor, skirting the perimeter in search of another door—not another entrance, those have all been sealed, but maybe one leading to a sub-level or a basement or cellar or something that might have a window or air duct or, at the very least, might provide some protection from what that second rumble signals.

The third rumble doesn't remain a rumble for long as artillery blasts through the structure towards the section of the facility I know the Praedari to have their Keeper "quarry" cornered, by now, or nearly found. Tomas likely among them but I don't have time to count the screams. The accelerant laid down catches fire quickly, following large loops as it spreads where gasoline was sloshed.

The first blast is more concentrated than what will come, intended to take out as many from the herd as possible—the next blasts are smaller in impact but spread out, machine gun bursts compared to shotgun blasts. As I run to take cover behind some concrete pillars I see a sub-room within this one with a metal sheet on a roller serving to curtain a window like one might see in a school cafeteria. I divert my path. A few tugs up on the metal curtain and it rolls up with a loud groan revealing a windowless office. I cuss but someone grabs my shoulder.

I turn and snarl, the heat of the spreading flames as they swallow accelerant and metal and debris hurting my face. Brittany yells something but the words are swallowed by the next blast. We both duck and she makes the signal for *follow me*.

We run to the staircase Tomas ascended, ducking as chunks of concrete and beams rain down on us. She holds up five fingers and looking up I see what she means: the fifth floor of four floors—the catwalk. From there, with help, one could get through the skylight. Of course, one has to make it there first, two of the three catwalks having collapsed already, one just whizzing past us to land by the entrance.

We're to the fourth floor when I hear the screams of whomever is left. I pause to look but Brittany grabs my arm and drags me up the narrow set of stairs to the catwalk. Wider than a beam but by no means generous, narrow passage rocks with our weight. I steady myself on a handrail and follow Brittany to the now glass-less skylight. She crouches and motions for me to climb up and with one fluid motion she hoists me high enough that I can pull myself the rest of the way through. Once through, I lay on my stomach and extend a hand down to her.

She shakes her head.

"Come on!"

She shakes her head again and points to her throat. Taking advantage of the lull between blasts, she shouts, "You have the Stone of Nyx—you can survive the jump and the moat of flames they laid down out there. I can't."

I bite my lip and reach for her again, out of instinct more than logic—my packsister who came back for me and showed me to safety. Instead of grabbing my hand, she fidgets with her hair before tossing something up to me: a hairpin, small enough that were it not for the heightened senses of the Everlasting I wouldn't have seen it, much less caught it.

I nod and she takes off running, back into the collapsing building now thick with smoke. I rush to the edge of the roof and see the flames. Four and a half stories, not such a bad fall for one of us, but the flames—so high that the circling drone has to keep enough distance to render it useless. I clutch the Stone of Nyx in my hand a moment, close my eyes, and kiss it.

I retreat a few paces, then run for the edge of the roof, leaping just as a tank lets loose another blast. I kick my legs to help gain distance, unsure if it matters but willing to risk it. Without looking back I feel the building behind me finally start to buckle, collapsing onto itself—and anyone still inside—with a heavy sigh.

I land in flames, engulfed like the metal skeleton of the building I just lept from, my sigh a grunt-cry and then shrieking as I feel my legs snap with the impact. A different heat than the fire starts at my throat as the Stone of Nyx starts glowing. I drag myself away from the building through the flames using my arms until I feel the magic mend the bones in my legs, then I stand and run, my skin already bubbling and popping by the time I emerge from the flames.

Then I see the tanks. I spin around to stare at the heap of rubble as it's engulfed in flames. No wailing of fire engine, of police, of ambulance; just the crackling and popping of flame.

"Delilah!" I am not even turned around when strong arms embrace me. The familiar scent of leather and wood and spices overpowers the stink of my own charred flesh. Zeke. "Where's Brittany?" he asks after a long hug, pulling away to survey my injuries.

"She didn't make it."

In that moment I realize my clothes are charred but also that I'm still clutching the hairpin she tossed to me, my body shielding it as though it were something precious while the Stone of Nyx protected *me*. I hold my clenched fist out to him and unfurl my fingers, the hairpin resting on my palm, unscathed.

"She was—"

"—one of us, yes," he finishes, taking the tiny metal shape from me. "A Keeper operative."

"And you knew?"

Zeke nods. "This contains *everything*," he explains. "This kept her connected to her handler—innocuous, isn't it?" he asks, holding the hairpin between two fingers. "No one would notice it, let alone suspect it if they did. It looks like every other one she wore and you and me and Tomas and the others? We couldn't choose it from fifty like it, not with a microscope. That's the magic of it, the extraordinary in the ordinary. Let this be a lesson to you, Delilah: things are never as they seem."

"Why didn't you tell me?" I accuse.

"We never spoke of it. We never spoke of any of our involvement, not like me and you do. Operatives go into this assuming they'll be living in a vacuum."

"But—she died."

"Yes, and so did the suicide bomber the packs hunted tonight."

"Yeah, but he *knew* he was going to die tonight. Brittany died because . . . to protect *me*."

"She knew what I knew: that her time as an operative was coming to an end—she couldn't maintain her cover as 'the survivor' for much longer without earning some suspicion. She gave her life for *this*, Delilah, not for *you*. It's all about timing," he says, wrapping his arm around my shoulders.

31

Now

I DON'T KNOW IF THERE'S A WORD FOR IT IN ENGLISH, or any language for that matter—when you can feel someone's reaction to something without having to see or hear it. I feel two jaws drop in near-simultaneity, the quickening of their hearts.

"*Armed?*" Victor asks.

I nod.

"Run!" yells one of the two remaining teens, the boy. To be honest, I thought about shouting the same and dragging them with me.

The girl reaches the hall first but stops short, the boy struggling to not run her over. She starts taking steps backwards, her hands up as if in surrender. The boy stumbles and retreats as well, able to see what Victor and I cannot.

The riddle not unanswered for long, Liam and Mina appear in the doorway, demonstrating again their uncanny knack for turning up to create someone else's worst case scenario.

"What have we here? A field trip?" Liam asks, his voice a grin but his jaw set.

Grunts, cursing, the snapping of wood and the clattering of it across the floor. I stand and take a step back towards the open patio door, moonlight illuminating the brawl. I'm trying to make sense of whose what is where when Mina holds a boy and a girl each up by their collar, a sharpened bit of wood lodged in the surface tissue of her thigh and one a bit deeper in the left breast—perhaps only millimeters from her dead heart. Her brother, unscathed, stands at her side. The metallic of blood thick in the air, but not Mina's; no, a quick scan of the two kids shows bloodied lips and blackening eyes. Each struggles against the body of their bondage.

"Maybe I should show you just where the heart *is*," Mina hisses, licking her lips at the girl with the wild hair.

"What should we do with them, boss?" Liam asks.

"Moving that body sure worked up an appetite," Mina suggests.

Victor looks to me, then to the now-crowded doorway. His gaze lingers on the two kids, each in turn, ending at last on the scrawnier of the two boys whom Liam restrains.

"You—Hunter," he points to the boy. "Liam, take him to the cellar."

"You mean where *she* is?!" Mina asks, handing the boy over to her brother. The corners of her mouth tugging up into a smile. "You *know* she's hungry . . . "

The two teens exchange frantic looks. Tears roll from the girl's eyes, splattering on the arm of Mina who now has her in a headlock. She sobs. Her and the boy start protesting, beginnings of angry utterances interrupting middles interrupting ends, crescendo-ing—but it's just noise to me as I study Victor in my peripheral vision. Who—or what—is he hiding in the cellar? Did Zeke really give up Ismae the Bloody to the Praedari like Quinn said? Why? What's going to happen to this boy? But even the gravity of these questions couldn't anchor my thoughts in the present. My spine lights up with familiar electricity as our almost-kiss replays in my mind.

The lights kick on, snapping me to the scene playing out before me—first noticeable in the hall, then in sections in the large open space that used to be a living room, then outside, like dominos. The artificial light drowns out the moonlight that streams in, as if the moon herself must wash her hands of this at once.

"Mina, take the girl back to her suite. The security system should be online again."

She nods in response.

"Hunter! No!" Kiley screams. "You *monster!*" she spits at Victor. "Hunter, hang in there! I'll get you out!" she encourages with a sob. "People will come looking for us, you know! You won't get away with this! They'll come for us, they'll find us!" she threatens, struggling against Mina.

And again their duet of argument and consolation and empty threats fills the room and filters out the patio door into the night, alternating between pleas and threats, promises and sobbing.

"It was Charlie's idea!" the boy cries after what feels like several moments, kicking against Liam. "It was her idea! Why aren't you trying to find her? Lock her up, not me!"

A hush falls over the girl who glares at him.

"Is that true?" Victor asks of the two.

No one responds. No one breathes.

Then: "Yes," the girl says, taking a deep breath.

It's a smart strategy, I credit her that now even if I didn't realize it at the time. If one of them might survive captivity away from the others, it would be Charlie; if one of them might break out of captivity on their own, it would be her. Of course, another way of looking at it would reveal it wise to keep their strongest asset accessible to the group, maximizing their collective potential for success. They think like Praedari, like packmates.

"I see," Victor starts, pausing a moment in apparent reflection. "Then let this be a lesson to all of you: your actions here matter. If you won't cooperate for your own sake, maybe this will teach you to cooperate for the sake of one another."

Hunter catches my eye and I realize that he hasn't spoken to me since my betrayal, despite his flinging accusations and excuses and reasons like spinning tires flinging mud.

"You," he spits. "You backstabbing, bloodsucking—" Victor cuts him off, barking instructions at Liam and Mina, but I can't look away.

I watch as Liam drags Hunter out of the room and into the hall. I watch as Mina follows, arrows still sticking out of her thigh and chest, likely from the blond girl and her friend who got away. She follows, holding the girl with the wild hair by the collar. Shoulders hunched, looking at the floor, the girl lets herself be dragged. She shakes with sobs as they disappear deeper into the facility. She pulls a crudely carved shank of wood from her sweatshirt and lets it clatter to the ground.

A trail of blood droplets behind them like bread crumbs except they won't be finding home tonight.

32

Now

A PUNISHMENT AS OLD AS THE EVERLASTING, BUT enhanced in modern nights. Near dawn inside the converted silo, the Praedari gather in front of a large, white screen that's been borrowed from the medical wing of the facility, used for presentations, mostly, but sometimes for movies. The Ritemaster, who translated the opening of Rite of the Howling, stands next to it, feet planted firmly, hands behind his back, eyes trained forward, face expressionless despite the excited din rising and echoing in the space. Projected onto the screen, the familiar landscape of the plot of land to the rear of the property behind the silo, alight in the sinking glow of a now-waning moon almost dipped below the horizon. A single, thick post, about half the height of an electric pole has been erected.

A funeral pyre.

The Ritemaster stands, waiting, shirtless, muscled and dark and wearing the same bloody war paint from the first night of the Howling. Those assembled inside can almost smell the stale blood on him. Two cloaked figures guide two others by their upper arms, tugging them through the overgrown grass, following the same track of beaten-down foliage the pole was likely dragged along. Red hair and strong statures in echo of one another, Liam and Mina each yank their arm from their captor and stride in the same measured gait towards the post, jaws set, unflinching.

The Ritemaster holds his hand up as they reach him, a gesture meant to stop them and it does. The two guides step towards the captives intending to restrain, but the Ritemaster shakes his head and they step back.

Inside the silo, the translator takes a half-step forward and an expectant hush falls over those assembled. The Ritemaster speaks to Liam and Mina, echoed inside the silo by the translator.

"We Praedari have many Rites—many revelatory, and a few that are not, but that are nonetheless necessary. Tonight we gather on the last night of the Howling to honor the decree of one of our alphas. At his request, we witness the Ritus Solis Ortus, the Rite of Sunrise. Liam and Mina, have you chosen which of you shall receive the punishment?"

Inside the silo, money changes hands as some take bets. Others made theirs the night before, some the night Victor made his intentions known.

The two step forward and clasp hands.

They speak in unison: "I will."

Inside the silo, something like an audible void where a gasp should be fills the space as the gathered Praedari begin to whisper amongst themselves. A few howl in glee; they'd bet on this outcome, and the odds weren't good.

The Ritemaster pauses for just one beat before tilting his head down and addressing the two again. "As you wish," the translator speaks as echo. Then, the Ritemaster to the two guides: "Bind them," again echoed by the translator.

He nods to the two guides who step towards Liam and Mina, producing chains from within the folds of the billowing cloaks that obscure their features.

"I will not be bound as a dog by a leash," Liam spits. "We are *Praedari*. Children of Sigurd, grand-children of Sighild, great-grandchildren of Ragnhild, and thus our lineage continues. Pure of blood, fierce of heart, Blooded and Bonded in honor. We, loyal Praedari, since the first of our Bloodline, until the last," he sings out in an accented lilt.

Still holding his sister's hand, the two cross to the post and position themselves in what would be back-to-back, but with the pyre between them. They clasp their free hands together, as if restraining one another. The guides pause before shrugging and turning to join their brothers and sisters in the converted silo-cum-theater. They leave one heavy, weathered barn door open enough that someone could slip through without struggle, but all eyes remain locked on the screen. Some look solemn, others grin, but all lean forward to hear better.

"Here we are, Sister," Liam states calmly.

"Here we are, Brother," Mina echoes. "Who do you think will scream first?"

"Scream? I'll be laughing all the way to Valhalla!" Liam boasts with the bark of a too-loud laugh.

"You think you'll be joining me at the table then, do you?" Mina fires back, furrowing her brow and biting her lip a moment, out of sight of her brother who faces the other direction.

"Joining *you*?" he starts, his voice catching in his throat. "Sister, the table we will sit at has been reserved for me and mine since the dawn of time," he continues.

"It has been a while since I've seen a sunrise, Brother," she offers, her voice softening.

The pitch-navy of nighttime lifts where the sun

hasn't yet broken over the horizon, an orange-green glow lurking behind mountain like a monster in a closet.

"It shall be easier to find our way, Sister, with all that light," he reassures her, squeezing her hands. Tears well up in her eyes, spill over. He feels her nod behind him.

The sun climbs higher, its first rays sneaking from behind peaks as smoke starts to rise from their skin. She squeezes his hands in return, as much to reassure as to restrain. She feels his muscles tense behind her, her predator within nearly leaping from her throat as her fangs slide forward.

"Lo, there do I see my Father and, Lo, there do I see my Mother, and Lo, there do I see my Brothers and Sisters," the two begin to intone in unison.

The smoking turns to sizzling and Liam drops his sister's hands. The two link arms at the elbows, struggling against the pyre, the other's strength and movement reinforcing the lock of their arms that holds their backs flush against the post. Both flail and writhe, teeth gnashing. The Ritemaster, skin bubbling and popping, darts for the silo to join his Brothers and Sisters in the safety offered by the structure. As quickly as he disappears from the projection screen he wriggles in the cracked-open barn door and heaves it shut.

Through gritted teeth, the two outside continue their prayer, more growl than human: "Lo, there do I see my people back to the beginning, and Lo, they do call to me . . . "

Liam's chest catches aflame first, three syllables ahead of his sister's but her voice chants loudly enough for them both when he screams, and his does the same to cover where hers falters. Hearing his sister's screams, tears slip from his eyes and burn a trail down each cheek.

" . . . and bid me take my place among them in the halls of Valhalla . . . " Their prayer-screams rise in the dawn to greet the sun, as if calling it into being, its brilliance humbled by the blaze of undead flesh on the pyre.

" . . . where the brave will live forev—!"

The final syllable is swallowed by the sound of a raven cawing.